Final Lap

Etienne Psaila

Final Lap

Copyright © 2024 by Etienne Psaila. All rights reserved.

First Edition: **December 2024**

No part of this publication may be reproduced, distributed, or transmitted in any form or by any means, including photocopying, recording, or other electronic or mechanical methods, without the prior written permission of the publisher, except in the case of brief quotations embodied in critical reviews and certain other non-commercial uses permitted by copyright law.

ISBN: 978-1-923393-12-7

Table of Contents

Chapter 1: The Roar of the Engines
Chapter 2: A Glimpse of Glory
Chapter 3: Behind the Visor
Chapter 4: The Arrival
Chapter 5: Unseen Sabotage
Chapter 6: The Whispering Gallery
Chapter 7: A Friend in the Shadows
Chapter 8: The First Confrontation
Chapter 9: A Night at the Gala
Chapter 10: Secrets Unveiled
Chapter 11: The Crash
Chapter 12: Echoes of Danger
Chapter 13: Under Pressure
Chapter 14: Old Allies
Chapter 15: The Hidden Workshop
Chapter 16: Crossroads
Chapter 17: The Setup
Chapter 18: Race Against Time
Chapter 19: The Decoy
Chapter 20: The Unraveling
Chapter 21: The Pursuit
Chapter 22: Collision
Chapter 23: The Final Race
Chapter 24: Exposed
Chapter 25: The Aftermath
Chapter 26: Healing Wounds
Chapter 27: New Horizons
Chapter 28: The Open Road

Chapter 1: The Roar of the Engines

Jake Turner stood at the edge of the racetrack, the scent of burnt rubber and high-octane fuel filling the air. The sun cast a golden hue over the asphalt, shimmering waves of heat distorting the distant grandstands. The cacophony of revving engines and clattering tools was music to his ears—a symphony of speed and precision.

"Jake! You gonna stand there daydreaming or help me with this transmission?" called out Max, his crew chief and oldest friend. Max's gruff voice cut through the noise, bringing Jake back to the moment.

"On it!" Jake replied, jogging over to their garage bay where their car—*The Phoenix*—gleamed under fluorescent lights. It wasn't the most expensive machine in the paddock, but what it lacked in funding, it made up for in heart and raw potential.

Their crew was a patchwork family of misfits: Sarah, the sharp-witted engineer who could tweak an engine to purr like a kitten or roar like a lion; Luis, the tire specialist with an uncanny ability to predict track conditions; and Emma, the strategist whose calm demeanor belied a mind that worked five moves ahead.

"Transmission's acting up again?" Jake asked, wiping his hands on a rag as he joined Max under the car.

"Just a little hiccup," Max grunted. "She's temperamental, but she'll hold."

Jake slid beneath the chassis, the cool metal pressing against his back. "We've got to make sure everything's perfect. First race is in two days."

Max glanced at him, a hint of concern in his eyes. "I know what's at stake, Jake. We all do."

Jake nodded, his expression hardening. This season was more than just another shot at glory; it was a chance to prove himself in a world that had written him off. Sponsors were scarce, and the big teams saw him as nothing more than a stepping stone. But he had something they didn't—an unyielding determination and a crew that believed in him.

As they worked, the sounds of other teams prepping echoed around them. Nearby, the Solaris Racing Team unloaded their brand-new cars—sleek, aerodynamic beasts funded by deep pockets. Their drivers strutted about in pristine suits, confidence oozing from every pore.

"Looks like the competition's stepping up their game," Sarah remarked, joining them with a tablet in hand. "They've got the latest tech—active suspension, adaptive aerodynamics."

Jake glanced over, unfazed. "All the fancy gadgets in the world won't make up for skill and teamwork."

"That's the spirit," Luis chimed in, rolling over a fresh set of tires. "Besides, I've got a feeling about this season."

They shared a moment of camaraderie, the unspoken understanding that they were in this together, come what may.

Later that evening, as the sun dipped below the horizon, casting long shadows across the track, Jake lingered beside *The Phoenix*. The garage was quiet now, his crew having called it a night. He ran his fingers along the car's fender, the cool metal smooth under his touch.

"Talking to her again?" came a voice from behind.

Jake turned to see Emma approaching, two steaming cups of coffee in hand. "She listens better than most people," he joked, accepting the cup.

They stood in comfortable silence, watching as the stars began to emerge in the night sky.

"Do you ever wonder if it's all worth it?" Emma asked softly.

Jake took a sip, considering the question. "Every day. But then I get behind the wheel, and everything makes sense. The world narrows down to just me, the car, and the track. Nothing else matters."

She nodded, her gaze distant. "I believe in you, you know. We all do."

He smiled appreciatively. "Couldn't ask for a better team."

A sudden burst of laughter broke the quiet as a group of rival drivers walked past the garage, their voices carrying a hint of mockery.

"Better get used to seeing our taillights, Turner!" one of them jeered.

Jake stiffened, but Emma placed a reassuring hand on his arm. "Ignore them. They'll eat their words soon enough."

"Let them talk," he replied, his jaw set. "We'll do our talking on the track."

As the night deepened, Jake finally headed home, navigating the winding roads leading away from the circuit. His modest apartment overlooked the city—a sprawling maze of lights and life. He leaned on the balcony railing, the weight of expectations pressing heavily upon him.

Flashes of memories flickered through his mind: his father's disappointed gaze when Jake chose racing over the family business; the countless doors slammed in his face by sponsors seeking more marketable faces; the near misses and mechanical failures that had plagued his previous seasons.

But beneath the doubt lurked a burning fire—a relentless drive to defy the odds.

His phone buzzed, jolting him from his thoughts. A message from an unknown number flashed on the screen.

"Watch your back this season. Not everyone plays fair."

A chill ran down his spine. He stared at the words, a sense of unease creeping in. Before he could process it further, another message appeared.

"This is just the beginning."

He tried calling the number, but it went straight to voicemail. Was this some kind of prank? Or a genuine warning?

The city lights suddenly seemed dimmer, the shadows deeper. Jake couldn't shake the feeling that unseen eyes were watching, that gears were turning behind the scenes in ways he couldn't yet comprehend.

He took a deep breath, steeling himself. Whatever challenges lay ahead, he was determined to face them head-on.

Back at the garage, a figure slipped out from behind *The Phoenix*, eyes glinting in the darkness. A small device was nestled in their gloved hand—a transmitter blinking with a tiny red light.

The race had yet to begin, but the game was already in motion.

Chapter 2: A Glimpse of Glory

The deafening roar of the crowd surged like a tidal wave as the cars lined up on the grid. The sun blazed overhead, reflecting off the vibrant paint jobs of the machines poised for battle. Jake sat in *The Phoenix*, hands gripping the steering wheel, heart pounding in rhythm with the thrum of the engine.

"All systems are green," Sarah's voice crackled through his earpiece. "Remember, steady on the first lap. Let the tires warm up."

"Got it," Jake replied, eyes fixed on the starting lights ahead. Beside him, the elite drivers of the circuit revved their engines—Adrian Cole, Marcus Valdez, and Lena Petrov, each a seasoned competitor with championship titles under their belts.

"Thirty seconds to start," Emma's calm tone interjected. "Stay focused, Jake. This is your race."

He took a deep breath, the world narrowing to the strip of asphalt ahead. The starting lights flickered from red to green, and in an instant, the cars lurched forward, tires screeching against the track.

The first corner was a melee of metal and speed. Jake maneuvered deftly, slipping between two rivals as they jostled for position. The G-forces pressed against him, but he moved with instinctual precision, *The Phoenix* responding to his every command.

By lap ten, he had climbed from his starting position at ninth to fifth place. The crowd began to buzz with murmurs of surprise—this underdog was making waves.

"You're doing great, Jake!" Luis exclaimed over the radio. "Keep this pace, and you'll catch Valdez."

Ahead, Marcus Valdez's car hugged the curves, but Jake noticed a slight hesitation on the tighter turns.

"He's struggling with oversteer," Jake muttered.

"Confirmed," Sarah responded. "His rear alignment might be off. Opportunity at turn six."

Jake pressed the accelerator, engine roaring as he closed the gap. At turn six, he feinted left before darting right, slipping past Valdez with millimeters to spare.

"Yes!" Max shouted. "That's fourth place!"

The race continued, each lap a blur of speed and strategy. Drivers peeled off for pit stops, but Emma's calculations had them holding out.

"Push for two more laps, then pit," she instructed.

As the leaders began to show signs of tire degradation, Jake maintained his pace. By the time he pitted, he had moved into third.

The pit stop was seamless—a ballet of coordinated movements as the crew swapped tires and refueled in seconds.

"Go, go, go!" Max yelled, slapping the side of the car as Jake sped off.

Rejoining the race, he found himself neck and neck with Lena Petrov. They battled fiercely, trading positions with every lap. The tension was palpable, the crowd on their feet.

On the final lap, Jake saw his chance. Lena took a defensive line, but Jake anticipated her move. He took the outside at turn twelve, braking later than seemed possible. Tires squealed, and for a heart-stopping moment, it looked like he might lose control. But *The Phoenix* held firm.

He surged ahead into second place, the finish line approaching fast. Adrian Cole was too far ahead to catch, but as Jake crossed the line, the realization of his achievement hit him.

"Second place, Jake!" Emma's voice was elated. "You did it!"

The team erupted into cheers as he pulled into the cooldown lap. Mechanics and crew members hugged and high-fived, the underdog team having defied expectations.

In the post-race press conference, flashes of cameras blinded him as reporters shouted questions.

"Jake, how does it feel to podium in the season opener?"

"Did you expect to perform this well against such strong competition?"

"What's next for Turner Racing?"

Jake smiled humbly. "It was a team effort. Couldn't have done it without my crew. We're just getting started."

Amidst the chaos, he caught sight of Adrian Cole, who regarded him with a measured gaze before offering a nod of acknowledgment. It was a small gesture, but it spoke volumes.

As the media frenzy subsided, a representative from Titan Motors approached him—a sleek man in an even sleeker suit.

"Mr. Turner, congratulations on your performance. We'd like to discuss potential opportunities."

Jake was taken aback. Titan Motors was one of the top teams, their resources unmatched.

"Thank you, but I'm committed to my team," he replied cautiously.

"Of course," the man smiled, handing over a business card. "But consider what we can offer. The door is open."

Returning to the garage, Jake found his team celebrating with bottles of cheap champagne, their faces alight with joy.

"You were incredible out there!" Sarah exclaimed, wrapping him in a hug.

"To Jake!" Max toasted, and they all raised their plastic cups.

But as the festivities continued, Jake couldn't shake a nagging feeling. Across the paddock, he noticed members of other teams casting glances his way—some curious, others less friendly.

In a quiet corner, Emma approached him. "Enjoying the moment?"

"Trying to," he admitted. "But something feels off."

She followed his gaze. "Success brings attention—both good and bad. We need to stay vigilant."

He nodded, the memory of the anonymous warning still fresh in his mind.

Later that night, as the team packed up, Jake received another message.

"Impressive performance. Be careful who you trust."

He looked around, searching for any sign of who might be sending these cryptic notes, but the paddock was nearly empty.

Unsettled, he slipped the phone back into his pocket. The thrill of victory was now tinged with unease. The shadows around him seemed to deepen, whispers of unseen threats lurking just beyond his sight.

Chapter 3: Behind the Visor

The early morning light filtered through the blinds of Jake's modest apartment, casting slatted patterns across the room. He sat at the small kitchen table, a bowl of cereal untouched before him. His mind replayed the race, every turn and maneuver dissected and analyzed.

A stack of mail lay nearby, bills mingling with letters. One envelope, marked with his father's law firm's insignia, caught his eye. He hesitated before opening it.

Jake, the letter began in his father's precise handwriting.

"I saw the race. Congratulations on your placement. It's not too late to reconsider joining the firm. Your talents could be put to better use in a stable profession. Think about your future."

He sighed, folding the letter carefully before setting it aside. The same argument, the same veiled disappointment.

His phone buzzed with a call from his mother.

"Hi, Mom," he answered, forcing cheerfulness into his voice.

"Jacob! I saw you on TV! You looked so handsome up there," she gushed.

"Thanks, Mom."

"Your father is proud, even if he doesn't say it," she continued gently.

He rubbed his temples. "We just have different views on what's important."

"Well, you know he worries. Racing is so dangerous. We just

want you to be safe."

"I know," he conceded. "But this is what I love."

She sighed softly. "Just promise me you'll be careful."

"I will. I always am."

After hanging up, he prepared to head to the team's workshop. The city streets were busy, the world moving at its relentless pace. As he rode his motorcycle through traffic, memories flooded back—his first karting race at age ten, the exhilaration of speed, the freedom it offered.

His father had never approved. Edward Turner was a man of structure and order, a successful attorney with a plan for his only son. But Jake had rebelled, drawn to the visceral allure of racing.

At the workshop, the atmosphere was buzzing. The team was already hard at work analyzing data from the race.

"Morning, Jake!" Luis called out. "Got some tweaks that'll shave milliseconds off your lap times."

"Every bit counts," Jake smiled.

He joined Sarah at the computer station. "What have we got?"

"Reviewing telemetry," she replied, eyes scanning the screens. "Your cornering speeds are impressive, but we're losing time on the straights. We need more power."

"Not easy without a bigger budget," he noted.

"Actually," Max interjected, approaching them. "I might have a lead on some new sponsors."

"Really?" Jake raised an eyebrow.

Max nodded, though his expression was cautious. "It's a smaller company, but they're eager to invest."

"That's great news," Sarah exclaimed.

"Set up a meeting," Jake agreed. "We need all the help we can get."

As the day progressed, Jake found himself growing restless. The anonymous messages weighed on him. Deciding to clear his head, he headed out for a run along the river.

The rhythmic pounding of his feet against the pavement helped to quiet his thoughts. The cityscape gave way to a park, the greenery a welcome respite.

"Nice day for a run," a voice called out.

He turned to see Lily Chen jogging beside him, earbuds dangling around her neck.

"Lily, right?" he recalled, recognizing the journalist who often covered the races.

"Good memory," she smiled. "Congrats on the podium finish."

"Thanks."

They fell into stride together.

"Working on a story?" he asked.

"Always," she replied cryptically. "Actually, I was hoping to get a quote from you."

"About?"

"Your sudden rise. Some say it's luck, others talent. What do you think?"

He chuckled. "Maybe a bit of both."

She studied him thoughtfully. "Off the record, have you noticed anything... unusual lately?"

He glanced at her, intrigued. "What do you mean?"

"Just... whispers of things happening behind the scenes. Drivers being approached with questionable offers."

A memory flashed of the messages he'd received. "Can't say I have," he lied cautiously.

She nodded, not pressing further. "Well, if you hear anything, let me know. I think there's more going on than meets the eye."

They parted ways, but her words lingered. Was she connected to the warnings?

That evening, Jake visited his father's house, a sprawling estate that contrasted sharply with his own modest living. The door was answered by their long-time housekeeper, Mrs. Delgado.

"Jacob! It's been too long," she greeted warmly.

"Hi, Mrs. D. Is my father in?"

"He's in his study."

Jake navigated the familiar halls, memories of his childhood surfacing with each step. He found his father behind a large mahogany desk, surrounded by legal texts.

"Jake," Edward acknowledged without looking up.

"Got your letter," Jake began.

Edward removed his glasses, setting them aside. "And?"

"And I'm not quitting racing."

A heavy silence settled between them.

"You have potential beyond this... hobby," his father stated.

"It's not a hobby. It's my career."

"A career with no stability, no safety."

"I'm doing what I love. Why can't you accept that?"

Edward stood, his gaze stern. "Because I don't want to see you throw your life away."

"Is that what you think I'm doing?" Jake's frustration bubbled over. "Maybe if you came to a race, you'd understand."

"I have responsibilities here," Edward deflected.

"No, you have excuses."

They stared at each other, the chasm between them widening.

"Fine," Jake relented. "I just wanted you to know that I'm not changing my mind."

As he turned to leave, his father spoke softly. "Your mother worries about you."

"I know," he replied without turning back. "Tell her I'm being careful."

Outside, the night air was cool against his skin. He took a deep breath, trying to release the tension.

His phone vibrated—a new message.

"They won't stop until they get what they want. Stay alert."

Frustration turned to anger. He dialed the number, but again, no answer.

"Who are you?" he muttered.

The next day at the track, Jake threw himself into practice. He pushed *The Phoenix* harder than ever, the car responding to his every demand.

"You're overdriving," Emma cautioned over the radio.

"I need to be faster," he insisted.

"Not at the expense of control. Bring it in."

Reluctantly, he returned to the pit lane. Max approached, concern etched on his face.

"What's going on, Jake?"

"Just dealing with some stuff," he admitted.

"Well, channel it constructively. We need you at your best."

He nodded, but his thoughts were elsewhere.

As the team packed up for the day, Jake noticed a sleek black car parked nearby. A man leaned against it, watching him intently.

"Can I help you?" Jake called out.

The man smiled thinly. "Just admiring your skills. You're quite the driver."

"Do I know you?"

"Not yet. Name's Victor Reynolds. I represent certain... interested parties."

Jake's guard went up. "Not interested."

"Now, now," Victor chuckled. "No need to be hasty. Opportunities are knocking."

"Find someone else."

Victor's expression hardened ever so slightly. "Think about it. We could make your dreams come true."

As Victor drove away, Jake felt a knot tighten in his stomach. The pieces were falling into place, and he didn't like the picture they were forming.

Returning to the garage, he found Lily waiting.

"We need to talk," she said urgently.

"About?"

"Victor Reynolds approached you, didn't he?"

He hesitated before nodding. "You know him?"

"Unfortunately. He's bad news. Tied to illegal betting syndicates and race fixing."

Jake's eyes widened. "Why are you telling me this?"

"Because you're in danger. They're targeting you."

He ran a hand through his hair, the weight of the situation pressing down. "What do they want from me?"

"To control the outcome of races. And they'll use any means necessary."

"Why me?"

"Because you're the wildcard—the variable they can't predict."

Jake took a deep breath. "What do we do?"

She met his gaze firmly. "We expose them. Together."

At that moment, the path ahead became clear. The race was no longer just about the checkered flag; it was about uncovering the truth and protecting everything he held dear.

Chapter 4: The Arrival

The morning sky was a canvas of swirling grays, threatening rain as Jake pulled into the paddock. The atmosphere was unusually electric, a buzz of anticipation rippling through the teams. Mechanics hurried about, whispers and glances exchanged with a mix of excitement and trepidation.

"What's with all the commotion?" Jake asked as he joined his crew in the garage.

Max looked up from his clipboard, his expression a blend of awe and concern. "You haven't heard? Adrian Cole is joining the circuit."

"Adrian Cole?" Jake repeated, the name heavy on his tongue.

"Yes, *the* Adrian Cole," Sarah interjected, eyes wide. "Three-time international champion, media darling, and racing prodigy."

Jake felt a knot tighten in his stomach. Adrian Cole was a legend—a driver whose skill was matched only by his enigmatic persona. His unexpected entry into their circuit was monumental.

"Why would he come here?" Jake wondered aloud.

"Maybe he's looking for new challenges," Emma suggested, though her tone betrayed uncertainty. "Or maybe there's more to it."

As if on cue, a convoy of sleek trailers emblazoned with the Cole Racing emblem rolled into the paddock. Photographers and journalists swarmed like bees to honey, flashes of cameras illuminating the overcast day.

"Well, there goes our quiet season," Luis quipped, attempting to lighten the mood.

Jake watched as Adrian emerged from one of the trailers—a tall figure clad in a tailored racing suit, his helmet tucked casually under his arm. His chiseled features and piercing blue eyes commanded attention, every movement exuding confidence.

"He's certainly not one to shy away from the spotlight," Jake remarked.

"Can you blame him?" Sarah replied. "With his record, he's earned it."

As the day progressed, the media frenzy intensified. Reporters jockeyed for interviews, and social media buzzed with speculation about Adrian's reasons for joining the circuit.

"Jake Turner!" a voice called out.

He turned to see Lily Chen approaching, microphone in hand and a cameraman in tow.

"Mind if I ask a few questions?" she inquired.

"Sure, why not," he agreed, though his attention remained divided.

"How do you feel about Adrian Cole joining the circuit?" Lily began.

"It's always exciting to have new talent," Jake replied diplomatically.

"Do you see him as competition?"

"Everyone on the track is competition," he smiled faintly. "But I focus on my own performance."

Behind them, Adrian was surrounded by a throng of admirers. He caught Jake's eye and offered a nod, a subtle acknowledgment that sent a ripple of unease through him.

"Seems he already knows who you are," Lily observed, following Jake's gaze.

"Maybe," Jake shrugged. "But we've never met."

"Well, with your recent performance, you're on everyone's radar."

The rest of the day was a blur of practice sessions and team meetings. Despite his efforts to concentrate, Jake couldn't shake the feeling that Adrian's arrival was more than just a coincidence.

Later, as dusk settled, Jake decided to introduce himself. He found Adrian alone by the track, gazing out over the empty stands.

"Adrian Cole?" Jake approached cautiously.

Adrian turned, a slight smile curving his lips. "And you must be Jake Turner. Congratulations on your podium finish."

"Thanks," Jake replied, extending his hand. "Welcome to the circuit."

Adrian shook it firmly. "Appreciate it. I've heard good things about you."

"Likewise," Jake said, though he couldn't read Adrian's intentions.

They stood in silence for a moment, the hum of distant generators the only sound.

"So, what brings you here?" Jake ventured.

Adrian's eyes flickered with something unreadable. "Change of scenery. New challenges. You know how it is."

"Sure," Jake nodded, though he sensed there was more to the story.

"Tell me," Adrian continued, his tone casual yet probing. "How are you finding the competition here?"

"It's fierce," Jake admitted. "But that's what makes it exciting."

Adrian chuckled softly. "Indeed. Though I've found that the real competition isn't always on the track."

Before Jake could respond, Adrian's manager appeared—a sharp-faced man with an air of impatience.

"Adrian, we need to go over the schedule," he said curtly, barely acknowledging Jake.

"Of course," Adrian replied. He glanced back at Jake. "We'll be seeing more of each other, I'm sure."

As they walked away, Jake couldn't shake the feeling that their encounter had been a calculated move.

Back at the garage, the team was wrapping up for the day.

"How'd it go with the superstar?" Max asked.

"Interesting," Jake replied thoughtfully. "He seems... different."

"Different how?" Emma probed.

"Hard to say. Like he's sizing things up."

"Well, keep your guard up," Max advised. "We don't need any distractions."

That night, Jake poured over race footage of Adrian's past performances. The man was undeniably skilled—his driving style aggressive yet precise, his strategies unpredictable.

A notification pinged on his laptop—an email from an anonymous sender.

"Watch out for those who hide behind friendly faces."

Jake's pulse quickened. Another cryptic message. Was this about Adrian? Or someone else?

He decided to forward the message to Lily.

Received another anonymous tip. Any thoughts?

A reply came swiftly.

Be careful. Meet me tomorrow. We need to talk.

The next day, as Jake headed to the track, he couldn't shake the sense of being watched. Shadows seemed longer, conversations hushed as he approached.

"Jake!" Lily called out, catching up to him near the hospitality tents.

"What's going on?" he asked.

She glanced around before speaking. "I've been digging. Adrian's move here is raising flags."

"What kind of flags?"

"Financial irregularities with his previous team. Sudden sponsorship changes. And get this—Victor Reynolds is involved."

Jake's jaw tightened. "Reynolds again."

"There's more," she continued. "Rumors are circulating that Adrian's arrival is part of a larger scheme to manipulate race outcomes."

"Are you saying he's working with Reynolds?"

"It's possible. Or he could be a pawn in a bigger game."

Just then, Adrian appeared, his gaze locking onto Jake and Lily. He approached with an easy smile.

"Good morning," Adrian greeted. "I see you're already busy with interviews."

"Just catching up," Jake replied evenly.

Adrian nodded, his eyes flicking between them. "Ms. Chen, always digging for a story."

"That's my job," Lily replied, her tone measured.

"Well, perhaps I can make it easier for you," Adrian offered. "An exclusive interview?"

"That would be appreciated," she responded cautiously.

"Excellent. I'll have my manager arrange it." He turned to Jake. "Best of luck in the practice session."

"Same to you," Jake said, watching as Adrian walked away.

"He's certainly... forward," Lily remarked.

"He's up to something," Jake muttered.

Practice that day was intense. Adrian's lap times were blisteringly fast, setting new records and pushing other drivers to their limits.

"He's in a league of his own," Sarah admitted, monitoring the data.

"Then we'll just have to step up," Jake declared.

As he pushed *The Phoenix* onto the track, determination fueled his every move. He matched Adrian's pace, each lap shaving precious milliseconds off his time.

But as he approached turn eight, the steering felt off—a slight delay that could be disastrous at high speeds.

"Something's wrong," Jake reported. "Steering's sluggish."

"Bring it in," Max ordered.

In the garage, the team examined the car.

"Steering linkage is loose," Luis observed, frowning. "That's odd. We checked everything this morning."

"Could it have been tampered with?" Emma asked quietly.

A heavy silence fell.

"Security footage," Jake suggested. "We need to review it."

As they waited for the footage, Jake's mind raced. Was someone trying to sabotage him? Or was it mere coincidence?

The video revealed a shadowy figure entering the garage during a shift change. Their face obscured, they moved with purpose, tools in hand.

"Can you enhance it?" Jake asked.

"I'm trying," Sarah replied, her fingers flying over the keyboard.

The image clarified just enough to make out a distinctive emblem on the person's jacket—a stylized letter "C."

"Cole Racing," Jake whispered.

"That's Adrian's team," Max growled. "This can't be happening."

"Hold on," Emma cautioned. "We can't jump to conclusions. It could be someone trying to frame them."

"Either way, we need to report this," Jake insisted.

They brought the evidence to the race officials, who promised an investigation. But Jake couldn't shake the feeling that they were now entangled in a dangerous game.

That evening, Jake received a message from Adrian.

"I heard about your car troubles. Hope everything is alright."

It was a simple message, but the undertone was clear.

"He knows," Jake said aloud.

"Knows what?" Emma asked, appearing at his side.

"About the sabotage. He's taunting me."

"Then we need to be smarter," she replied firmly. "Stay focused. Don't let him get inside your head."

Jake nodded, appreciating her steadfast support.

As the next race day loomed, tensions escalated. The paddock was abuzz with rumors, alliances shifting like sand.

Lily approached Jake once more. "Be careful tomorrow. I have a feeling things are going to escalate."

"Any new information?" he asked.

"Nothing concrete, but the atmosphere is... volatile."

The night before the race, Jake found himself alone on the empty track. The silence was profound, the stands towering above like silent sentinels.

He closed his eyes, taking a deep breath. He needed clarity, focus.

Footsteps echoed behind him.

"Couldn't sleep either?" Adrian's voice cut through the stillness.

Jake turned to face him. "Just clearing my head."

"A lot on your mind?" Adrian probed.

"You could say that."

Adrian stepped closer. "You know, Jake, we're not so different. Both driven, both seeking something more."

"Is that so?"

"Join me," Adrian offered suddenly. "Together, we could dominate this circuit."

Jake studied him, searching for hidden motives. "What exactly are you proposing?"

"An alliance. We help each other out, ensure mutual success."

"And what about fair competition?"

Adrian's smile was cold. "Fairness is a construct for the naïve. Winners make their own rules."

"Thanks, but I'll pass," Jake replied firmly.

Adrian's eyes hardened. "Think carefully, Jake. Opportunities like this don't come often."

"I'd rather earn my victories."

A tense silence settled between them.

"Very well," Adrian said finally. "But remember, every choice has consequences."

As Adrian walked away, Jake felt a chill run down his spine.

Returning to the garage, he found a small envelope tucked under the door. Inside was a single photograph—a picture of *The Phoenix* engulfed in flames.

On the back, a message read:

"Back down, or everything burns."

Jake's hands trembled ever so slightly. The threat was real, and the stakes had just been raised.

He knew now that he was facing not just competition on the track, but a dangerous adversary willing to do whatever it took to win.

The race was no longer just about speed and skill—it was a battle for survival.

Chapter 5: Unseen Sabotage

The sun peeked over the horizon, casting a golden glow across the racetrack as the teams prepared for the day's practice sessions. Jake arrived early, hoping to find solace in the quiet hum of the waking circuit. He approached *The Phoenix*, its sleek form gleaming under the fluorescent lights of the garage.

"Morning, Jake," Sarah greeted him, already immersed in data analysis. "I've tweaked the engine mapping—you should feel a smoother power delivery out of the corners."

"Sounds good," he replied, donning his racing suit. "Let's see how she runs."

As he settled into the cockpit, a familiar sense of unity washed over him—the melding of man and machine. The engine roared to life, and he guided the car onto the track. The first few laps felt solid; the adjustments made a noticeable difference.

But on the fifth lap, as he accelerated down the back straight, a sudden jolt rattled through the car. The steering became heavy, and the engine sputtered briefly before regaining power.

"Did you feel that?" Jake radioed in, concern edging his voice.

"Data shows a momentary drop in fuel pressure," Sarah responded. "Bring it in; we'll check it out."

Back in the garage, the team swarmed over *The Phoenix*, diagnostic tools in hand.

"Fuel pump seems fine," Luis muttered, scratching his head.

"No apparent issues."

"Maybe a sensor glitch," Max suggested. "But let's run a full systems check to be safe."

They cleared him to return to the track, but the uneasy feeling lingered. On his next run, the brakes felt spongy entering turn four, forcing him to adjust his line to avoid spinning out.

"Something's wrong with the brakes now," Jake reported, his frustration mounting.

"That's impossible," Sarah exclaimed. "We just replaced the brake pads and bled the lines yesterday."

"Bring it back," Max ordered tersely.

As the crew delved deeper into the mechanical anomalies, Jake paced the garage. Each issue seemed unrelated, yet the timing was suspicious.

"Could it be sabotage?" Emma whispered, voicing the question on everyone's mind.

"Who would do that?" Luis asked incredulously. "And how? We have security protocols."

Jake thought back to the shadowy figure caught on camera days before, the emblem of Cole Racing emblazoned on their jacket. His encounter with Adrian, the veiled threats—it all pointed to something more sinister at play.

"Double-check everything," Jake instructed. "And I mean everything. If someone is tampering with the car, we need to find out how."

As the team inspected every component, Jake stepped

outside for fresh air. The paddock was alive with activity, but beneath the surface, an undercurrent of tension simmered.

"Problems?" a voice drawled behind him.

Jake turned to see Victor Reynolds leaning casually against a wall, a sly smile on his face.

"What do you want?" Jake asked coldly.

"Just expressing concern," Victor replied smoothly. "Heard you've been having some technical difficulties."

"We're handling it."

Victor's eyes gleamed with a predatory light. "You know, these kinds of setbacks can be... discouraging. But there are ways to ensure smooth sailing."

"I'm not interested in your offers."

"Come now, Jake. Success doesn't have to be a struggle. With the right alliances, doors open."

Jake stepped closer, his gaze steely. "I earn my victories. I don't buy them."

Victor's smile faded slightly. "Suit yourself. But remember, pride can be costly."

As Victor sauntered away, Jake's resolve hardened. He returned to the garage to find Sarah holding a small device in her gloved hand.

"What's that?" he asked.

She looked up, her expression grim. "A transmitter. I found it attached to the wiring harness. It's been interfering with the car's systems."

"Someone planted it?" Max exclaimed, anger flaring.

"Looks that way," Sarah confirmed. "It's sophisticated—not something you pick up at a hardware store."

Jake clenched his fists. "We need to report this to the officials."

They presented the device to the race authorities, but the response was disappointingly tepid.

"We'll look into it," the official said dismissively. "But without concrete evidence pointing to a culprit, there's not much we can do."

Frustrated, the team regrouped in their trailer.

"This can't continue," Emma declared. "We need to tighten security."

"I'll set up surveillance," Luis offered. "Motion sensors, cameras—the works."

"Good," Jake agreed. "And we'll implement a check-in system. No one enters the garage without authorization."

As the day wore on, the weight of the situation pressed heavily upon them. Trust was eroding, and the joy of racing was overshadowed by suspicion.

That evening, Jake met with Lily at a quiet café away from the circuit.

"I heard about the sabotage," she said, concern evident in her eyes. "Are you okay?"

"Been better," he admitted. "Someone's trying to undermine us."

"Any idea who?"

"Could be Adrian's team. Or Reynolds. Maybe both."

Lily leaned in, lowering her voice. "I did some digging. There's chatter about a group manipulating race outcomes for profit. Drivers, teams, even officials might be involved."

"That's a serious accusation."

"I know. But the patterns are there—unexpected mechanical failures, underdog wins that shift betting odds significantly."

Jake sighed, running a hand through his hair. "So we're caught in the middle of a conspiracy."

"Seems that way. But if we can gather enough evidence, we can expose them."

"At what cost?" he mused. "They're already playing dirty."

She reached across the table, her hand brushing his. "You're not alone in this. We'll find a way."

A flicker of warmth sparked between them, but the moment was interrupted by the ring of her phone. She glanced at the screen and frowned.

"Everything okay?" Jake asked.

"Just a tip," she said, though her tone suggested more. "I'll follow up later."

As they parted ways, Jake couldn't shake the feeling that time was running out.

Back at his apartment, he received another message from the unknown sender.

"They're closing in. Trust no one."

He stared at the words, a chill settling over him. The walls seemed to close in, the shadows deepening.

Sleep came fitfully, haunted by dreams of crashing cars and faceless adversaries.

The next morning, he arrived at the track to find his team huddled around *The Phoenix*.

"What's wrong?" he asked, heart sinking.

"The engine won't start," Sarah said, frustration etched on her face. "We've checked everything—battery, starter, ignition. It's like it's dead."

"Another sabotage?" Luis speculated.

"Possibly," Max growled. "But we don't have time to waste."

They worked feverishly, stripping the car down to its core components. Hours passed with no solution in sight.

"We might have to withdraw from the practice session," Emma said quietly.

"No," Jake insisted. "We can't let them win."

"Jake, we're out of options," Max replied. "Unless a miracle happens, we won't make it."

Just then, a delivery arrived—a crate labeled with no sender. Cautiously, they opened it to find a brand-new ignition system compatible with *The Phoenix*.

"Where did this come from?" Sarah asked, bewildered.

A note fluttered to the ground.

"Use this. Keep fighting."

"Is this another trap?" Luis wondered.

Jake examined the equipment. "It looks legitimate."

"We don't have much choice," Max conceded. "Install it."

With the new ignition in place, the engine roared to life.

"Unbelievable," Sarah muttered.

"Who would help us anonymously?" Emma questioned.

"Maybe we have an ally," Jake suggested, though doubt lingered.

They made it to the practice session with minutes to spare. On the track, Jake pushed *The Phoenix* harder than ever, determined to reclaim control.

But as he rounded the final corner, a flash of movement caught his eye—a figure on the sidelines aiming something towards the car.

A loud pop sounded, and the rear tire exploded, sending the car spinning out of control.

"Jake! What's happening?" Sarah's voice screamed over the radio.

He fought the steering, managing to bring the car to a skidding halt just before the barriers.

"Rear tire blew," he gasped, adrenaline coursing through him. "I think someone shot it out."

"Get back here now," Max ordered urgently.

As safety crews rushed to his aid, Jake scanned the crowd but saw no sign of the culprit.

Back in the garage, the atmosphere was tense.

"This is escalating," Emma stated. "We need protection."

"I'm going to the officials again," Max declared. "They can't ignore this."

But deep down, Jake knew that the official channels might not be enough. The unseen enemy was growing bolder, and the line between competition and warfare was blurring.

He resolved then that he would uncover the truth, no matter the cost.

Chapter 6: The Whispering Gallery

The rain came down in sheets, casting a somber mood over the paddock. The rhythmic drumming on the metal roofs provided a stark backdrop to the hushed conversations that filled the air.

Jake moved through the labyrinth of trailers and tents, the hood of his jacket pulled low to shield against the downpour. He was heading to a meeting with Lily, who had urgently requested to see him.

As he passed by the Solaris Racing tent, he caught snippets of a heated discussion.

"...can't keep this up," a voice hissed. "If they find out about the modifications, we're finished."

"Relax," another voice replied. "Everyone's doing it. As long as we stay under the radar, it's fine."

Jake paused, his curiosity piqued. Illegal modifications? He edged closer, careful to remain unseen.

"Did you hear about Turner's team?" the first voice continued. "They're becoming a problem."

"Not for long," the second voice chuckled darkly. "Plans are in motion."

A shiver ran down Jake's spine. He retreated silently, the gravity of the situation intensifying.

He met Lily in a secluded corner of the hospitality area, away from prying eyes.

"Thanks for coming," she said, her expression grave.

"What's going on?" he asked.

"I've uncovered more information," she whispered, sliding a folder towards him. "There are multiple teams involved in using illegal modifications—enhancements that give them an unfair advantage."

Jake flipped through the documents, his eyes widening at the detailed reports and schematics.

"How did you get this?" he questioned.

"I have sources," she replied evasively. "But that's not all. There's a secret network facilitating these modifications and ensuring they pass inspections unnoticed."

"And the officials?"

"Some are complicit, others are oblivious. It's a web of corruption."

Jake exhaled slowly. "I overheard a conversation earlier. Teams are worried about being exposed."

"Which means they're desperate," Lily pointed out. "Desperate people do dangerous things."

He thought of the recent sabotage attempts, the escalating threats. "They're trying to eliminate any variables—anyone who could disrupt their scheme."

"Exactly," she nodded. "We need to act before it's too late."

"How? We can't just accuse them without solid proof."

She tapped the folder. "This is a start. But we need more—

something irrefutable."

An idea sparked in Jake's mind. "What if we could catch them in the act?"

"That's risky," she cautioned. "But it might be our only option."

"There's a drivers' meeting tonight," he recalled. "Maybe we can gather intel there."

They agreed to reconvene after the meeting. As Jake made his way to the conference room, he couldn't shake the feeling of being watched.

The meeting was held in a spacious hall, the walls adorned with racing memorabilia. Drivers and team representatives milled about, their conversations a low murmur.

Adrian Cole stood at the center, effortlessly commanding attention. He caught Jake's eye and offered a sly smile.

"Good evening, everyone," the race director began, calling the room to order. "We have several important topics to discuss, including safety protocols and upcoming schedule changes."

As the meeting progressed, Jake scanned the faces around him. Some appeared tense, others indifferent. He noticed Victor Reynolds standing at the back, his gaze fixed intently on the proceedings.

"Now, onto technical regulations," the director continued. "There have been rumors of non-compliance regarding vehicle specifications. Let me remind you that any violations will result in severe penalties."

A ripple of unease passed through the crowd.

"Are there any questions?" the director asked.

Silence hung heavy in the air.

"Very well. Meeting adjourned."

As the attendees dispersed, Jake lingered near a side exit. He saw a group of team managers, including those from Solaris Racing and Cole Racing, slip into a private room.

Driven by urgency, he stealthily approached the door, which was ajar just enough to allow voices to carry.

"...we can't afford any more mistakes," a stern voice declared. "The spotlight is turning towards us."

"Our modifications are undetectable," another insisted. "The inspectors haven't caught on."

"But Turner's team is digging," a third voice warned. "And that journalist—she's a liability."

Jake's heart pounded. They were discussing him and Lily.

"Then we handle them," the stern voice asserted. "Accidents happen all the time in this sport."

A cold dread settled over Jake. He needed to warn Lily and his team immediately.

As he turned to leave, the door creaked loudly. The voices inside fell silent.

"Who's there?" someone barked.

Without waiting, Jake bolted down the corridor, footsteps echoing behind him.

"Stop!" a voice shouted.

He raced through the maze of hallways, bursting out into the rain-soaked night. The downpour masked his movements as he weaved between trailers.

He ducked behind a stack of tires, holding his breath as shadows passed by.

"Find him!" the stern voice ordered. "He can't have gone far."

Once the footsteps receded, Jake made his way back to his team's garage, soaked and shaken.

"Jake! What happened?" Emma exclaimed upon seeing him.

"No time to explain," he panted. "We need to secure the garage and alert everyone. We're in danger."

He quickly relayed what he had overheard.

"This is serious," Max said grimly. "We need to contact the authorities."

"With what proof?" Sarah countered. "It's their word against ours."

"Then we gather proof," Jake declared. "But we have to be careful."

They agreed to keep a low profile and increase security measures.

Jake tried calling Lily, but the call went straight to voicemail.

"She mentioned following a lead," he told the team. "I'm worried about her."

"Try her again later," Emma suggested. "For now, we need to focus."

As night deepened, the team worked tirelessly, double-checking equipment and setting up surveillance.

Around midnight, Jake received a text from an unknown number.

"You can't hide forever."

He showed the message to the team.

"They're trying to intimidate us," Luis said angrily.

"Well, it's working," Sarah admitted, her voice trembling slightly.

"We can't let fear control us," Jake insisted. "That's what they want."

Just then, a noise outside caught their attention—the sound of metal clattering.

"Did you hear that?" Emma whispered.

They armed themselves with tools and cautiously stepped outside. The rain had eased, but the ground was slick and visibility low.

A figure darted between shadows.

"There!" Max pointed.

They gave chase, but the intruder was swift, disappearing into the darkness.

"Check the cars," Jake ordered.

Returning to the garage, they found *The Phoenix* untouched, but the spare parts storage had been ransacked.

"They're trying to sabotage our resources," Sarah surmised.

"This is escalating too quickly," Emma said. "We need help."

"Agreed," Jake nodded. "First thing in the morning, we'll go to the racing commission."

Exhausted, the team settled in for the night, taking turns keeping watch.

At dawn, Jake finally reached Lily.

"Thank goodness," he sighed in relief. "Are you okay?"

"Yes," she replied, though her voice was strained. "I had to lay low. I think I'm being followed."

"They know we're onto them," he informed her. "We need to be careful."

"I have evidence," she revealed. "Recordings, documents—enough to expose them."

"That's great news," he said, hope stirring. "We should meet somewhere safe."

"Agreed. I'll send you a location."

They arranged to meet at a public park later that day.

Before leaving, Jake and his team compiled all the information they had gathered. With Lily's evidence, they would have a compelling case.

As Jake headed to the meeting spot, he remained vigilant,

scanning for any signs of danger.

Lily arrived, clutching a folder tightly.

"Here it is," she said, handing it over. "This should be enough to bring them down."

He leafed through the contents—emails implicating team officials, audio recordings of incriminating conversations.

"This is incredible," he breathed. "We need to get this to the authorities immediately."

"Agreed," she said. "But we have to be discreet."

As they made their way back to the parking lot, a black van screeched to a halt in front of them. Masked men emerged, blocking their path.

"Run!" Jake shouted, grabbing Lily's hand.

They sprinted across the park, adrenaline fueling their escape. The men pursued relentlessly.

Spotting a crowded market ahead, Jake led them into the throng of people, weaving through stalls and patrons.

"Split up," he urged. "We'll meet at the team's garage."

She hesitated but nodded, disappearing into the crowd.

Jake dodged down an alley, the sounds of pursuit fading. He circled back towards the circuit, his mind racing.

Upon reaching the garage, he found the team already on high alert.

"Where's Lily?" Emma asked anxiously.

"She should be here soon," he replied, catching his breath.

Minutes felt like hours as they waited. Finally, Lily stumbled in, visibly shaken but unharmed.

"They're getting bolder," she said between gasps. "We need to act now."

They compiled all their evidence and contacted a trusted official known for integrity.

"Meet me at the commission office," the official instructed. "I'll ensure this is handled properly."

As they prepared to leave, a message blared over the circuit's public address system.

"All teams are to report to the main auditorium for an urgent meeting."

"This can't be good," Max muttered.

"Stay together," Jake advised. "And keep the evidence secure."

At the auditorium, the atmosphere was tense. The race director stood on the stage, flanked by security personnel.

"It has come to our attention that there are serious allegations regarding illegal activities within our circuit," he announced gravely. "An investigation is underway."

Whispers erupted among the attendees.

"We need to present our findings," Lily urged.

But before they could step forward, Victor Reynolds took the stage.

"Thank you, director," he began smoothly. "I regret to inform you all that certain individuals have been spreading false rumors, attempting to destabilize our esteemed organization."

He gestured towards Jake and Lily.

"These parties have fabricated evidence to undermine the integrity of the sport."

Gasps and murmurs filled the room.

"That's a lie!" Jake shouted, stepping forward. "You're the one behind the corruption."

"Please, Mr. Turner," Victor sneered. "Baseless accusations won't save you."

Security guards moved to intercept Jake and Lily.

"Hand over any so-called evidence," one guard demanded.

"Don't do it," Emma called out.

Amid the chaos, Adrian Cole emerged from the crowd.

"Wait," he said, holding up a hand. "Let them speak."

Victor's eyes narrowed. "Adrian, this doesn't concern you."

"On the contrary," Adrian replied coolly. "I believe it concerns all of us."

He turned to Jake. "If you have proof, now is the time to present it."

Seizing the opportunity, Jake stepped onto the stage.

"These documents expose a network of illegal modifications, race fixing, and sabotage orchestrated by Victor Reynolds and his associates," he declared, projecting the evidence onto a screen.

The room erupted in shock as emails, financial records, and recordings played out.

Faces blanched, and the accused teams began to panic.

"This is outrageous!" Victor bellowed. "It's all fabricated!"

But the weight of the evidence was undeniable.

The race director signaled the security personnel. "Detain Mr. Reynolds and anyone involved pending a full investigation."

As guards moved to apprehend Victor, he attempted to flee but was quickly subdued.

Relief washed over Jake and his team.

Adrian approached him, extending a hand. "Well done, Turner."

Jake accepted the handshake cautiously. "Why the change of heart?"

Adrian smiled wryly. "I may be competitive, but I believe in fair play. Besides, I despise cheaters."

Lily joined them, a triumphant glow in her eyes. "We did it."

"Thanks to you," Jake acknowledged. "Couldn't have done it alone."

The aftermath was a whirlwind of official statements, arrests, and media frenzy. The sport was shaken, but the path to restoring integrity had begun.

As the sun set, casting a golden hue over the track, Jake and his team gathered one last time.

"To truth and perseverance," Max toasted, raising a bottle of sparkling cider.

"To standing up for what's right," Emma added.

They clinked glasses, the tension of the past weeks giving way to a sense of accomplishment.

Jake glanced at Lily, their eyes meeting with unspoken understanding.

"What's next?" she asked softly.

He smiled. "Back to racing, the way it should be."

She grinned. "And maybe a well-deserved break?"

"Sounds good to me."

As they looked out over the empty stands, the future felt open and hopeful.

But Jake knew that challenges would always lie ahead. With his team by his side and integrity in his heart, he was ready to face whatever came next.

Chapter 7: A Friend in the Shadows

The city skyline shimmered under the pale glow of the moon, a tapestry of lights reflecting off the tranquil waters of the harbor. In a modest apartment overlooking the bustling streets below, Lily Chen sat hunched over her laptop, the screen casting a bluish hue over her determined features.

Stacks of documents, scribbled notes, and photographs cluttered her desk—a mosaic of clues that formed a dark picture of deceit and corruption within the racing world. Red lines connected faces to corporations, question marks hovering over key players. At the center of it all was a name circled multiple times: **Victor Reynolds**.

She rubbed her temples, fatigue gnawing at the edges of her focus. Months of undercover work had led her here, but the closer she got to the truth, the more dangerous her pursuit became.

A soft chime interrupted her thoughts—a notification flashing on the screen.

Encrypted message received.

She opened it cautiously. The anonymous tipster had been reliable so far, feeding her snippets of information that guided her investigation.

"They're onto you. Be careful."

Her heartbeat quickened. The risks were escalating, but backing down was not an option. She glanced at a photo pinned to the wall—a candid shot of Jake Turner, helmet under his arm, eyes steeled with determination.

Lily had first noticed Jake during his unexpected rise in the circuit. His defiance of the odds mirrored her own quest for truth. Perhaps he could be an ally, but trust was a luxury she couldn't afford easily.

The next day, the sun hung low in the sky as she navigated the crowded paddock. The scent of fuel and the symphony of engines formed a familiar backdrop. She spotted Jake by his team's garage, engrossed in conversation with his crew.

Taking a deep breath, she approached, her demeanor professional yet guarded.

"Jake Turner?" she called out.

He turned, his expression shifting from surprise to recognition. "Lily Chen, right? The journalist."

"Good memory," she replied with a faint smile.

"What can I do for you?"

She glanced around, ensuring they were out of earshot. "I was hoping we could talk—somewhere private."

Jake raised an eyebrow. "Sounds serious."

"It is."

He considered her for a moment before nodding. "There's a quiet spot behind the hospitality tents."

They walked in silence to a secluded area, the distant roar of practice laps muffled by the barriers.

"So, what's this about?" he asked, leaning casually against a railing.

Lily hesitated, choosing her words carefully. "I've been investigating certain... irregularities within the racing circuit. I believe you're entangled in something bigger than you realize."

Jake's gaze hardened slightly. "If this is about the sabotage and threats, I'm already aware that someone's targeting me."

"It's more than just you," she pressed. "There's a network of corruption—race fixing, illegal modifications, bribery. And powerful people are involved."

"Do you have proof?"

She pulled a folded document from her bag. "I've gathered evidence, but I need more. I think you can help me."

He unfolded the paper, scanning the contents. "Why come to me?"

"Because you're one of the few who hasn't been compromised. You're honest, and you have access to places I don't."

Jake sighed, handing back the document. "Look, I've got enough on my plate trying to keep my team afloat and staying alive."

"I understand the risks," she acknowledged. "But if we work together, we might stand a chance at exposing them."

He studied her intently. "How do I know I can trust you?"

She met his gaze unwaveringly. "You don't. Just like I don't know if I can trust you. But we both want the same thing—the truth."

A tense silence settled between them before Jake finally

spoke. "Alright. What do you need from me?"

Relief flickered across her face. "Keep your eyes and ears open. Anything unusual—conversations, behaviors, access to restricted areas—could be a lead."

He nodded slowly. "Fine. But we do this carefully. I won't put my team in danger."

"Agreed."

As they parted ways, Lily couldn't shake the feeling that forming this alliance was both a necessary step and a dangerous gamble.

Later that evening, Lily returned to her apartment, the city's nocturnal energy pulsing below. She settled at her desk, reviewing the day's findings. A new email awaited her, the sender anonymous.

"You're digging too deep. Stop, or there will be consequences."

Her blood ran cold. It was the first direct threat she'd received. She locked her doors and double-checked the security system, the shadows in her apartment seeming darker than before.

The next morning, she met with her editor, **Thomas Grant**, at a quiet café away from prying eyes.

"You're taking big risks, Lily," Thomas cautioned, concern etched on his face. "This story could make your career, but it could also end it."

"I'm aware," she replied, stirring her coffee absently. "But the truth needs to come out."

He leaned forward. "At least let me assign you a security detail."

She shook her head. "That would draw too much attention. I need to move freely."

Thomas sighed heavily. "Just promise me you'll be careful."

"I always am."

Leaving the café, Lily felt the weight of isolation pressing upon her. Trust was scarce, and allies were few. Her phone buzzed with a message from an unknown number.

"You're not alone. Help will come when needed."

She frowned, unsure whether to feel reassured or further unnerved.

Meanwhile, Jake grappled with his own doubts. The recent attempts on his car, the veiled threats, and now this collaboration with Lily—it all painted a picture of a dangerous game being played in the shadows.

He confided in Emma, his team's strategist, about the situation.

"Do you think it's wise to get involved?" she asked, concern evident.

"I don't see much choice," Jake replied. "If what Lily says is true, we're already involved whether we like it or not."

"Just promise me you'll be cautious," Emma urged. "We can't afford to lose you."

He offered a reassuring smile. "I will. And I won't let anything happen to the team."

As the days progressed, Lily and Jake exchanged information discreetly. She provided insights into the potential players involved in the corruption, while he relayed observations from within the paddock.

One evening, Jake spotted Victor Reynolds engaged in an intense conversation with Adrian Cole near the VIP lounge. The body language suggested tension, with Adrian appearing resistant.

Jake relayed the encounter to Lily.

"Interesting," she mused. "Adrian might not be as complicit as we thought. There could be factions within the network."

"Or he's just a better actor," Jake cautioned.

"Either way, it's worth investigating."

Their collaboration deepened, a cautious trust forming between them. Yet, both remained vigilant, aware that any misstep could have dire consequences.

One night, as Lily poured over documents, her laptop screen flickered before going black. A warning message flashed:

"Final warning. Cease your investigation."

Her heart pounded as she scrambled to check her files. Much of her data had been corrupted or deleted.

Panicking, she called Jake. "They've hacked into my system. I've lost most of the evidence."

"Can you recover it?" he asked urgently.

"I don't know. I need help."

"Meet me at the team's garage. We have secure systems there."

She arrived under the cover of darkness, her nerves frayed. Sarah, the team's engineer with a background in cybersecurity, set to work on salvaging the data.

"I can retrieve some of it," Sarah assured them. "But it might take time."

"Thank you," Lily said gratefully.

As they waited, Jake turned to her. "Maybe it's time to involve the authorities."

She shook her head vehemently. "Not yet. We don't know who we can trust. If the corruption runs as deep as we suspect, reporting this prematurely could backfire."

He conceded the point. "Alright. But we need a backup plan."

Sarah interrupted. "I've recovered partial files and traced the intrusion. It originated from a network associated with Reynolds Enterprises."

"Victor Reynolds," Jake muttered. "He's making his move."

Lily squared her shoulders. "Then we need to make ours."

Together, they devised a strategy to gather irrefutable evidence. Jake would attend an exclusive event where key figures would be present, using a concealed device to record conversations. Lily would work on securing any digital trails and reaching out to her anonymous tipster for additional leads.

As Jake prepared for the event, Emma approached him with a worried expression. "Are you sure about this?"

"No," he admitted. "But it's the best shot we have."

"Just promise me you'll be careful."

He smiled softly. "I will."

At the opulent gala, chandeliers cast a warm glow over the assembled elite of the racing world. Jake navigated the crowd, engaging in polite conversation while subtly steering discussions toward revealing topics.

He managed to corner **Stephen Blackwood**, a notorious team owner rumored to have ties to illicit activities.

"Quite the season we're having," Jake commented.

"Indeed," Stephen replied smoothly. "Unexpected upsets, thrilling races."

"Some might say too unexpected," Jake probed.

Stephen's eyes narrowed slightly. "Racing is full of surprises."

"True. But it's the surprises off the track that concern me."

Before Stephen could respond, Victor Reynolds appeared beside them. "Jake Turner, enjoying the evening?"

"Trying to," Jake replied evenly.

Victor smiled thinly. "Careful not to delve into matters that don't concern you. It can be... hazardous."

"Is that a threat?"

"A friendly warning."

Feeling the tension escalate, Jake excused himself, mingling back into the crowd.

Meanwhile, Lily received a message from her anonymous source.

"They know. Get out now."

Her heart raced as she tried to contact Jake, but the call wouldn't connect.

At the gala, Jake noticed security personnel converging subtly, their gazes darting toward him. Realizing he was compromised, he headed for the exit.

He slipped out into the night, weaving through the city's backstreets to avoid pursuit. Reaching the team's garage, he found Lily and the crew anxiously waiting.

"What happened?" Lily asked.

"I think they made me," he said breathlessly. "We need to move fast."

Sarah stepped forward. "I've intercepted communications indicating they're planning to eliminate any threats."

"Then we need to expose them now," Lily declared.

They consolidated all their gathered evidence, uploading it to multiple secure locations and sending copies to trusted media contacts and legal authorities.

As dawn broke, headlines exploded across news outlets:

"Massive Corruption Unveiled in Professional Racing: Illegal Modifications, Race Fixing Exposed."

Arrests were made swiftly. Victor Reynolds and several high-profile individuals were taken into custody. The racing commission announced a thorough investigation and immediate reforms.

In the aftermath, Jake and Lily found a moment of respite amidst the media storm.

"We did it," she said, a mixture of relief and disbelief.

"Couldn't have done it without you," he replied sincerely.

She smiled, a genuine warmth in her eyes. "I guess we make a good team."

"Maybe we should consider future collaborations," he suggested lightly.

"Perhaps," she agreed, a hint of teasing in her tone. "But hopefully under less perilous circumstances."

They shared a quiet laugh, the tension of the past weeks finally easing.

As the racing season resumed under renewed integrity, Jake's team thrived, their efforts recognized and respected.

Lily's exposé earned her acclaim, but more importantly, it upheld the truth she so fiercely pursued.

Their paths continued to cross, both professionally and personally, hinting at a deeper connection forged in the crucible of adversity.

Standing on the podium after another hard-fought race, Jake looked out over the cheering crowd. Among them, he spotted Lily, her eyes meeting his with a shared understanding.

The journey had been fraught with danger and uncertainty, but together they had emerged victorious—not just in racing, but in championing honesty and justice.

As the national anthem played and confetti filled the air, Jake felt a profound sense of fulfillment. The shadows had been illuminated, and the road ahead was bright.

Chapter 8: The First Confrontation

The morning sun cast long shadows across the paddock as Jake arrived at the team's garage, a knot of frustration tightening in his stomach. The previous night's revelations weighed heavily on his mind—the sabotage attempts, the mounting pressure, and the nagging suspicion that betrayal might be closer than he imagined.

He found Max hunched over a spread of blueprints, his brows furrowed in concentration.

"Morning, Jake," Max greeted without looking up. "Got some new ideas for the fuel injection system."

"That's great," Jake replied tersely, his gaze scanning the garage for **Tim Hawkins**, their lead mechanic. "Have you seen Tim?"

Max glanced up, sensing the tension. "He should be around here somewhere. Everything okay?"

"Not really," Jake admitted. "I need to talk to him about the car issues we've been having."

Max nodded slowly. "Let me know if you need anything."

Jake moved deeper into the garage, passing Sarah and Luis, who were engrossed in a technical discussion.

"Hey, Jake," Sarah called out. "We were just reviewing the telemetry data from the last session. Found some irregularities in the throttle response."

"Add it to the list," Jake muttered.

He spotted Tim at the back of the garage, tinkering with a set of tools. The mechanic was a stocky man with grease-stained hands and a perpetually unreadable expression.

"Tim, we need to talk," Jake said, approaching him.

Tim looked up, wiping his hands on a rag. "Sure thing, boss. What's on your mind?"

Jake folded his arms. "We've been experiencing a series of mechanical failures lately—steering issues, brake problems, engine sputters. It's becoming a pattern."

Tim shrugged nonchalantly. "Machines have quirks. We're pushing them hard out there."

"This isn't about quirks," Jake pressed. "These are critical failures that could have caused serious accidents. I need to know if there's something going on that I should be aware of."

Tim avoided his gaze, focusing instead on organizing his tools. "I've checked everything. The car's in top shape before it hits the track. Sometimes things happen that are out of our control."

"Tim," Jake's voice hardened. "I need straight answers. Are you sure nothing's been tampered with?"

Tim finally met his eyes, his expression guarded. "You're questioning my work?"

"I'm questioning the circumstances," Jake replied evenly. "I trust my team, but I need to be certain we're not missing anything."

Tim sighed, leaning against the workbench. "Look, Jake, I've been with you since the beginning. I want to see us win as much as you do. If there was something wrong, I'd tell you."

"Then help me understand why these issues keep occurring."

"Could be any number of things," Tim suggested. "Wear and tear, faulty parts from suppliers, maybe even driver error."

Jake bristled at the insinuation. "You think this is on me?"

"Didn't say that," Tim replied defensively. "Just covering all possibilities."

An uncomfortable silence settled between them.

"Is there anything else you want to tell me?" Jake asked, his gaze probing.

Tim shook his head. "No. But I'll double-check everything before the next session."

"Make sure you do," Jake said, turning to leave.

As he walked away, he couldn't shake the feeling that Tim was hiding something. The mechanic's evasiveness only fueled his suspicions.

He found Emma outside the garage, reviewing race strategies.

"Emma, we need to talk," he said quietly.

She looked up, concern flickering in her eyes. "What's wrong?"

"I'm starting to think someone on the inside might be sabotaging us."

Her expression hardened. "What makes you say that?"

"Tim's been acting strange. Every time we have a car issue,

he has an excuse. And he's not giving me straight answers."

Emma considered this. "That's a serious accusation. Do you really think he'd betray us?"

"I don't want to believe it," Jake admitted. "But the evidence is piling up."

"Maybe we should keep an eye on him," she suggested. "But we need to be careful. Accusing him without proof could fracture the team."

"I know," he agreed. "But we can't ignore this."

"Let's set up discreet surveillance," Emma proposed. "If there's foul play, we'll catch it."

"Good idea," Jake nodded. "I'll talk to Luis and Sarah."

As they re-entered the garage, Max approached them, his expression concerned.

"Everything alright?" he asked.

"Just discussing strategy," Jake replied.

Max studied him for a moment before nodding. "Let me know if you need anything."

Throughout the day, Jake couldn't help but watch Tim closely. Every glance, every movement seemed suspect. Was he being paranoid, or was there truly a traitor among them?

Later that afternoon, during a break in practice sessions, Jake received a text from an unknown number.

"Trust is a fragile thing. Be wary of those closest to you."

He showed the message to Emma. "It's starting again."

She frowned. "Someone's playing mind games."

"Or giving us a warning," Jake countered.

"Either way, we need to stay vigilant."

As the team gathered for a debrief, the atmosphere was strained. Tim avoided eye contact, focusing intently on his notes.

"Great work today, everyone," Jake began, forcing a smile. "Let's keep up the momentum."

After the meeting, Sarah pulled him aside. "I found something you should see."

She led him to her workstation, pulling up a series of data logs. "These are the engine diagnostics from the last three sessions. There's an anomaly here," she pointed to a spike in the readings. "It appears someone accessed the ECU and altered the fuel maps."

"Can you tell who did it?" Jake asked.

She shook her head. "Not without more digging. But access is limited to a few people."

"Tim included," Jake noted grimly.

"Yes," she confirmed.

"Keep this between us for now," he instructed. "I don't want to tip anyone off."

That evening, Jake sat alone in the dimly lit garage, the hum of the cooling units the only sound. He contemplated the path ahead. If Tim was involved, confronting him directly might push him further into secrecy—or worse, provoke retaliation.

He decided to take a different approach.

The next day, he approached Tim with a conciliatory tone.

"Hey, Tim. Sorry about the other day. Stress is getting to me."

Tim seemed surprised but relaxed slightly. "No worries. We all feel it."

"Maybe we can work together to figure out these issues," Jake suggested. "Your expertise is invaluable."

Tim nodded slowly. "Sure. Let's get to the bottom of it."

As they worked side by side, Jake observed him carefully, looking for any signs of deception. But Tim remained professional, offering insights and suggestions.

Perhaps he was wrong. Maybe Tim was innocent, and the true saboteur was someone else entirely.

But the seed of doubt had been planted, and trust was a luxury Jake could no longer afford.

Chapter 9: A Night at the Gala

The grand ballroom of the Regency Hotel glittered with opulence. Crystal chandeliers cast a warm glow over the elegantly dressed guests mingling beneath. The annual Racing Charity Gala was a highlight of the season—a night where rivalries were set aside in the name of philanthropy.

Jake adjusted the cuffs of his tailored suit, feeling slightly out of place amidst the extravagance. Emma had insisted he attend, both to represent the team and to network with potential sponsors.

"Relax," she whispered, linking her arm with his as they entered the room. "You clean up nicely."

He offered a wry smile. "I'd rather be in the garage."

"Tonight, you're a celebrity," she teased. "Enjoy it."

They navigated the crowd, exchanging pleasantries with familiar faces. Waiters circulated with trays of champagne and hors d'oeuvres, and a string quartet played softly in the background.

"Jake Turner," a voice called out.

He turned to see Adrian Cole approaching, a confident grin on his face.

"Adrian," Jake acknowledged.

"Didn't expect to see you here," Adrian remarked, eyeing him appraisingly. "You usually avoid these events."

"Decided to make an exception," Jake replied coolly.

"Glad you did," Adrian said, his tone dripping with insinuation. "It's good to step out of one's comfort zone."

Emma sensed the tension. "If you'll excuse me, I'll grab us some drinks," she said, leaving them alone.

Adrian watched her depart before leaning in slightly. "She's quite devoted to you."

"Emma's a valuable member of my team," Jake stated.

"Is that all?" Adrian smirked. "Seems there's more beneath the surface."

Jake's eyes narrowed. "What are you getting at?"

"Just observing," Adrian shrugged. "You know, Jake, we've had our differences, but perhaps it's time we put them aside."

"I'm listening," Jake said skeptically.

"I have an offer for you," Adrian began. "Join my team. With your skill and my resources, we could dominate the circuit."

Jake chuckled incredulously. "Why would I do that?"

"Because you're wasting your potential," Adrian pressed. "Stuck with a team that's holding you back."

"My team is the reason I'm here," Jake retorted. "I wouldn't abandon them."

Adrian's expression hardened. "Loyalty is admirable, but it doesn't win championships."

"I'll take my chances," Jake replied firmly.

"Think about it," Adrian insisted. "Opportunities like this

don't come often."

"Is this the part where you make veiled threats?" Jake challenged. "Because I've heard them before."

Adrian raised his hands defensively. "No threats. Just a proposition. But I warn you, the path you're on is fraught with obstacles."

"I'm not afraid of obstacles."

"Perhaps you should be," Adrian said quietly. "There are forces at play beyond your control."

Before Jake could respond, a voice interrupted them.

"Gentlemen, enjoying the evening?" Victor Reynolds appeared beside them, his eyes gleaming with calculated interest.

"Victor," Adrian greeted. "We were just discussing potential collaborations."

"Is that so?" Victor's gaze shifted to Jake. "I trust you're considering Adrian's offer seriously."

"I'm not interested," Jake said flatly.

Victor sighed theatrically. "A shame. We could accomplish great things together."

"Some things aren't for sale," Jake replied.

Victor's smile faded. "Stubbornness can be costly."

"Is that a threat?" Jake asked, echoing his earlier question to Adrian.

"Merely an observation," Victor said smoothly. "Success requires adaptability."

"Excuse me," Jake said, stepping away. "I have other people to speak with."

He walked briskly toward the balcony, needing fresh air. The encounter had left him agitated, and he needed to clear his head.

The cool night air was a welcome relief as he stepped outside. The city lights stretched out before him, a sea of twinkling possibilities.

"Mind if I join you?" a familiar voice asked.

He turned to see Lily Chen approaching, her evening gown shimmering under the moonlight.

"Be my guest," he said, managing a smile.

"You look like you could use some company," she observed.

"Just had a lovely chat with Adrian and Victor," he admitted. "They're persistent."

"I saw," she nodded. "What did they want?"

"To recruit me, apparently."

"Are you considering it?" she teased lightly.

"Not a chance."

"Good," she said approvingly. "They can't be trusted."

"I figured as much."

They stood in comfortable silence for a moment, the distant sounds of the gala muted.

"How's the investigation going?" he asked quietly.

"Making progress," she replied. "But it's like untangling a web—every thread leads to another."

"Be careful," he cautioned. "They're playing for keeps."

"I know," she said, her eyes reflecting a mix of determination and concern. "But so am I."

He admired her resolve. "We're in this together."

She smiled softly. "Yes, we are."

Their moment was interrupted by the sudden arrival of Adrian, his demeanor less composed than before.

"Am I interrupting?" he asked, though it was clear he didn't care.

"Actually, you are," Jake replied tersely.

Adrian ignored him, focusing on Lily. "Ms. Chen, I'd like to discuss an exclusive interview."

"I'm off the clock," she said politely. "Perhaps another time."

"I insist," Adrian pressed, his tone firm.

"She said no," Jake interjected, stepping between them.

Adrian's eyes flashed with irritation. "This doesn't concern you."

"Anything involving my friends concerns me."

Adrian smirked. "Always the hero."

"Better than being a bully," Jake shot back.

Adrian's composure slipped. "Watch yourself, Turner. You're out of your depth."

"Is that so?"

"You're playing a dangerous game," Adrian warned. "You don't know who you're dealing with."

"Why don't you enlighten me?" Jake challenged.

Before the confrontation could escalate further, Emma appeared, concern etched on her face.

"Is everything alright here?" she asked.

"Just a friendly conversation," Adrian said, regaining his composure. "Enjoy your evening."

He walked away, disappearing back into the crowd.

"That was intense," Lily remarked.

"He's hiding something," Jake said. "And I'm going to find out what."

Emma placed a hand on his arm. "Let's not cause a scene here."

"She's right," Lily agreed. "We need to be strategic."

Jake took a deep breath, nodding. "You're both right. I'm

letting him get under my skin."

"That's what he wants," Emma pointed out. "Don't give him the satisfaction."

"Come on," Lily suggested. "Let's get back inside."

As they rejoined the gala, Jake couldn't shake the feeling that lines had been drawn. Adrian's veiled threats and Victor's manipulations signaled a brewing storm.

He needed to be prepared.

The rest of the evening passed uneventfully, but the undercurrents of tension remained. Sponsors and officials approached Jake with polite interest, but he sensed ulterior motives lurking beneath their compliments.

As the gala drew to a close, Jake gathered his team.

"Let's head back," he said. "We've got work to do."

In the limousine ride back to the hotel, the team discussed the night's events.

"Adrian and Victor are up to something," Max observed. "We need to stay one step ahead."

"Agreed," Jake said. "Tomorrow, we focus on the car and tightening security."

"Do you think Tim is involved?" Sarah asked cautiously.

"I'm not sure," Jake admitted. "But we can't rule anything out."

Emma leaned forward. "We need to trust each other now more than ever."

He met her gaze. "I trust all of you. We'll get through this together."

Back at his hotel room, Jake stood by the window, gazing out at the city lights. The path ahead was fraught with uncertainty, but he was resolute.

A soft knock on the door pulled him from his thoughts.

He opened it to find a sealed envelope on the floor, no one in sight.

Picking it up, he unfolded the paper inside.

"You can't win. Stop trying."

He crumpled the note in his fist, a steely determination settling within him.

"Game on," he muttered to himself.

As he prepared for bed, he knew that the stakes had never been higher. The confrontation with Adrian had solidified his resolve.

Whatever challenges awaited, he was ready to face them head-on.

Chapter 10: Secrets Unveiled

The rain hammered against the windows of the small café where Jake and Lily had agreed to meet. The city outside was a blur of lights reflected on wet streets, the usual hustle muted by the downpour. Jake sat at a corner table, his fingers wrapped around a mug of untouched coffee, his mind replaying the events of the past few days.

He looked up as the door chimed, and Lily stepped in, shaking off her umbrella. Her eyes met his, a mix of urgency and concern evident in her gaze. She weaved through the scattered tables and slid into the seat across from him.

"Thanks for coming on such short notice," she said, lowering her voice.

"What's going on?" Jake asked, leaning forward. "Your message sounded serious."

"It is," she replied, pulling a slim folder from her bag. "I've uncovered something you need to see."

She handed him the folder, her hands slightly trembling. Jake opened it to reveal a series of documents—financial records, emails, and photographs. As he sifted through them, a knot formed in his stomach.

"These are transactions between Victor Reynolds and several teams," he noted, his eyes scanning the figures. "Large sums of money exchanged just before races."

"Exactly," Lily confirmed. "But it doesn't stop there. Look at the email correspondence."

Jake flipped to the printed emails, his eyes widening as he read. Messages discussing deliberate car malfunctions, strategic pit stop delays, and orchestrated crashes. Names of drivers and team members were mentioned—some he recognized, others less familiar.

"This is... this is race fixing," he said, disbelief tinged with anger. "They're manipulating the outcomes."

"Yes," Lily nodded. "And it's bigger than we thought. Multiple teams are involved, and the network stretches across the circuit."

Jake's mind raced. "Why hasn't this been exposed? How are they getting away with it?"

"Because they have insiders," she explained. "Officials, mechanics, even some drivers. They're all part of it, keeping it under wraps."

He sat back, the weight of the revelation pressing down on him. "And where do I fit into all this?"

Lily hesitated before speaking. "You've been outperforming expectations, Jake. You're an underdog disrupting their plans. According to some of the messages, they're seeing you as a threat."

He met her gaze, a mix of determination and fear flickering in his eyes. "They want to eliminate me."

"Yes," she admitted softly. "I believe you're their next target."

A tense silence settled between them, punctuated only by the rhythmic patter of rain against the glass.

"Why are you telling me this?" he finally asked.

"Because you deserve to know," she replied earnestly. "And because I need your help to expose them."

He ran a hand through his hair, processing the information. "How do we do that? They're powerful, connected. If we make a wrong move..."

"I've been collecting evidence," Lily said, her voice steady. "But I need more—something irrefutable that can bring them down. With your access and my resources, we can gather what we need."

Jake considered her proposal. The thought of going up against a clandestine network was daunting, but the alternative—allowing them to continue unchecked—was unacceptable.

"I'm in," he agreed. "But we have to be careful. We can't trust anyone."

She offered a small smile. "Agreed. We'll have to watch each other's backs."

They spent the next hour strategizing, mapping out key figures and potential vulnerabilities. As they spoke, the café began to empty, the late hour thinning the crowd.

"One more thing," Lily said, her tone serious. "I think someone on your team might be involved."

Jake's eyes narrowed. "What makes you say that?"

"In some of the communications, there's mention of inside information about your car and schedules," she explained. "They refer to a 'source' close to you."

He clenched his jaw, the possibility of betrayal cutting deep. "Do you know who?"

She shook her head. "Not yet. But we need to be cautious."

He nodded grimly. "I'll keep an eye out."

As they prepared to leave, Lily placed a hand on his arm. "Jake, I know this is a lot to take in. If you want to back out—"

"No," he interrupted firmly. "I won't let them get away with this. They need to be stopped."

She studied him for a moment, respect shining in her eyes. "Alright. Let's do this."

They parted ways outside the café, the rain having subsided to a light drizzle. Jake pulled up the hood of his jacket and made his way back to his car, his thoughts a whirlwind of concern and determination.

Driving through the slick streets, he replayed the details Lily had shared. The idea that someone on his team could be feeding information to their adversaries was a bitter pill to swallow. His mind immediately went to Tim, the mechanic whose vague reassurances had done little to quell his suspicions.

Arriving at the team's garage, Jake found it mostly deserted, the only light emanating from the workshop where Max was still tinkering with equipment.

"Burning the midnight oil?" Jake asked, stepping inside.

Max looked up, wiping his hands on a rag. "Couldn't sleep. Thought I'd make some adjustments to the suspension setup."

Jake managed a thin smile. "Always striving for perfection."

"That's the goal," Max chuckled, though his expression turned serious as he observed Jake's demeanor. "You okay? You look troubled."

He considered confiding in Max but decided against revealing too much. "Just a lot on my mind. The competition's heating up."

Max nodded knowingly. "It's a tough game. But we've got a solid team. We'll pull through."

"Speaking of the team," Jake began cautiously, "have you noticed anything... unusual lately? Anyone acting out of character?"

Max raised an eyebrow. "What do you mean?"

"Equipment going missing, unexpected visitors, that sort of thing."

"Can't say that I have," Max replied thoughtfully. "Is there something you're worried about?"

"Just being cautious," Jake deflected. "Can't afford any surprises."

"Understood," Max agreed. "I'll keep an eye out."

"Thanks," Jake said appreciatively. "I'm going to call it a night."

"Get some rest," Max advised. "We've got a big day tomorrow."

As Jake left the garage, he couldn't shake the feeling of unease. The shadows seemed deeper, the silence heavier. He checked his surroundings before getting into his car, half-expecting someone to emerge from the darkness.

The drive home was uneventful, but the weight of the conspiracy bore down on him. Once inside his apartment, he double-checked the locks and set the security alarm.

Paranoia, perhaps, but warranted under the circumstances.

He sat at his kitchen table, the documents from Lily spread out before him. Lines connected names and organizations, a web of deceit that threatened to ensnare him. His phone buzzed, startling him.

A text message from an unknown number:

"You're digging where you shouldn't. Stop now, or face the consequences."

A chill ran down his spine. They knew.

He quickly typed a response to Lily:

"Received a threat. They might be onto us. Be careful."

A reply came moments later:

"Got it. Stay safe. We'll regroup tomorrow."

Jake knew sleep would be elusive. He spent the next few hours backing up the evidence, storing copies in secure locations. If something happened to him, the truth would still come out.

As dawn approached, exhaustion finally overtook him. He collapsed onto the couch, drifting into a restless slumber filled with fragmented dreams of roaring engines and shadowy figures.

The next morning, Jake arrived at the racetrack earlier than usual. The air was crisp, the sky painted with the soft hues of sunrise. He made his way to the garage, determined to uncover the mole within his team.

He found Emma organizing equipment, her efficiency a constant in the midst of chaos.

"You're here early," she remarked with a smile.

"Couldn't sleep," he admitted.

"Everything alright?"

He hesitated before deciding to confide in her. "I need to tell you something, but it stays between us."

Her expression became serious. "Of course. What's going on?"

He glanced around to ensure they were alone. "Lily's uncovered evidence of race fixing. A network involving multiple teams and officials."

Emma's eyes widened. "That's huge. Do you have proof?"

He nodded. "Yes, but it gets worse. She thinks someone on our team is feeding them information."

She looked shocked. "Who?"

"I don't know yet," he confessed. "But we need to be careful."

She absorbed the information, her mind clearly racing. "What can I do to help?"

"Keep an eye out for anything suspicious," he instructed. "And trust no one."

"Understood," she affirmed. "We'll get to the bottom of this."

As the rest of the team trickled in, Jake observed them closely. Tim arrived, greeting everyone with his usual gruff demeanor. Sarah and Luis engaged in lighthearted banter as they set up their workstations.

"Morning, everyone," Jake called out, projecting an air of normalcy. "Let's have a great practice today."

They responded with enthusiasm, but beneath the surface, tension simmered.

Throughout the day, Jake monitored interactions, looking for any signs of deceit. During a break, he noticed Tim stepping away to take a phone call, speaking in hushed tones.

"Everything okay?" Jake asked casually as Tim returned.

"Yeah," Tim replied shortly. "Just handling some personal business."

Jake nodded, filing the moment away for later consideration.

During the afternoon session, an unexpected malfunction occurred—an issue with the fuel intake causing the engine to misfire. The team scrambled to diagnose the problem.

"That's strange," Sarah commented, examining the data. "We checked this system thoroughly."

"Could it be a faulty part?" Luis suggested.

"Possible, but unlikely," she replied. "These components are new."

Jake exchanged a glance with Emma, both of them thinking the same thing.

"Let's run a full diagnostic," Jake ordered. "I want to know exactly what's going on."

As they worked, Jake noticed Tim watching from a distance, his expression unreadable.

Later, when the garage had cleared out, Jake and Emma reviewed the diagnostic results.

"Look at this," she pointed to a line in the report. "Someone accessed the engine control unit last night and altered the settings."

"Who had access?" Jake asked.

"Aside from us, only Tim," she said grimly.

Jake felt a mix of betrayal and anger. "We need to confront him."

"Wait," Emma cautioned. "We need proof. If we accuse him without it, he could deny everything and cover his tracks."

"You're right," he agreed reluctantly. "But how do we get it?"

She thought for a moment. "We set a trap. Give him an opportunity to incriminate himself."

"How?"

"Let's plant some false information," she suggested. "Something only he would know. If it gets back to them, we'll have our answer."

He nodded. "It's risky, but it's worth a shot."

They devised a plan, creating a fake strategy document outlining a supposed new engine modification that would give them a significant advantage.

"Make sure it's convincing," Jake said as they prepared the

document.

"Don't worry," Emma assured him. "It'll be believable."

The next day, they left the document in a place where Tim would find it. Jake observed from a distance as Tim discovered the paper, glanced around, and discreetly pocketed it.

Now, all they could do was wait.

That evening, Jake met with Lily at a secure location—a small, quiet park away from prying eyes.

"I think we might have identified the leak," he told her, recounting the day's events.

"That's a significant breakthrough," she said. "If we can link him to the network, it'll strengthen our case."

"I just hate the idea of someone on my team betraying us," he admitted.

"It's never easy," she sympathized. "But we need to focus on the bigger picture."

"Agreed," he sighed. "What's our next move?"

"I've arranged a meeting with a contact who has insider information," she revealed. "He might be able to provide us with the final pieces of evidence we need."

"When is this meeting?"

"Tomorrow night," she replied. "But there's a catch—he insists on meeting alone."

Jake frowned. "That sounds dangerous."

"I can handle myself," she assured him. "But I appreciate your concern."

"At least let me be nearby," he insisted. "In case things go south."

She considered his offer. "Alright. But keep a low profile."

"Deal."

The following night, Lily headed to the rendezvous point—a dimly lit warehouse on the outskirts of the city. Jake parked a short distance away, keeping watch from his car.

Lily entered the building, her footsteps echoing in the vast space. A figure emerged from the shadows—a middle-aged man with a nervous demeanor.

"Are you Lily?" he asked cautiously.

"Yes," she confirmed. "You must be Daniel."

He nodded. "I don't have much time. If they find out I'm here..."

"Your information could make a real difference," she encouraged.

He handed her a flash drive. "This contains records of all transactions, communications, everything. It's the proof you need."

"Thank you," she said sincerely. "Why are you helping us?"

"I can't live with the guilt anymore," he confessed. "They've ruined lives, all for profit."

Before she could respond, the sound of tires screeching outside shattered the moment.

"What's that?" Daniel panicked.

Lily's heart raced. "We need to get out of here."

Jake watched in alarm as several vehicles pulled up to the warehouse, men pouring out and rushing inside.

He grabbed his phone, dialing Lily. "They're coming your way! Get out now!"

Inside, Lily and Daniel darted towards a side exit, but their path was blocked.

"Split up!" she urged. "They can't catch us both."

Daniel hesitated before nodding and fleeing in the opposite direction.

Lily dashed through the maze of crates and machinery, her pursuers closing in. She spotted a narrow passageway leading to a back door and made a beeline for it.

Bursting outside, she ran towards the street where Jake had parked. He saw her emerge and started the engine, pulling up alongside her.

"Get in!" he shouted.

She leaped into the car, and they sped away just as the men reached the curb.

"Are you okay?" he asked, adrenaline coursing through his

veins.

"Yes," she panted. "But Daniel..."

"We'll figure it out," he assured her. "Did you get the data?"

She held up the flash drive. "Right here."

"Then we have what we need."

As they put distance between themselves and the warehouse, Lily couldn't shake the worry for Daniel's safety.

"I hope he got away," she said quietly.

"Me too," Jake agreed. "But right now, we need to secure that information."

They drove to a safe location—a small office space Lily had rented under an alias. Once inside, they began reviewing the contents of the flash drive.

The data was extensive—detailed records of race manipulations, payouts, and communications between the conspirators. It was the smoking gun they needed.

"This is it," Lily said, a mix of relief and triumph in her voice. "We can bring them down."

"Not so fast," Jake cautioned. "We need to handle this carefully. If we go to the authorities, there's a chance they'll be tipped off."

"You're right," she agreed. "We need to make this public in a way they can't suppress."

"An exposé," he suggested. "Broadcast it widely."

"I can write the article," she said, determination shining in her eyes. "But we need to ensure it's disseminated through multiple channels."

"I have contacts who can help," Jake offered. "But we'll need to act quickly."

They spent the next several hours compiling the information, cross-referencing it with their previous findings, and preparing the report.

As dawn broke, exhaustion tugged at them, but the urgency of their mission kept them focused.

"Almost there," Lily said, typing furiously. "Just need to finalize a few details."

Suddenly, a loud crash sounded from the entrance—a door being forced open.

Jake sprang to his feet. "They're here!"

Lily grabbed the flash drive and stuffed it into her pocket. "We need to go, now!"

They raced towards the back exit, but footsteps thundered down the hallway.

"Split up," Jake instructed. "I'll distract them."

"No way," she protested. "We stick together."

"Trust me," he insisted. "I'll meet you outside."

Reluctantly, she nodded and slipped out a side door.

Jake faced the approaching footsteps, steeling himself. As the men burst into the room, he upended a table to block their path and darted down another corridor.

"After him!" one of them shouted.

He led them on a chase through the building, using his knowledge of the layout to stay ahead. Reaching a stairwell, he climbed to the roof, the cool morning air hitting his face.

He scanned the area below, spotting Lily safely making her way to the car.

"Thank God," he murmured.

But his relief was short-lived as the men emerged onto the roof.

"End of the line," one of them sneered.

Jake backed away, the edge of the roof pressing against his spine. "You don't have to do this."

"Orders are orders," the man replied, advancing.

Just then, sirens wailed in the distance—police cars approaching rapidly.

"Time to go," another man urged.

They retreated, disappearing back into the building.

Jake exhaled deeply, his heart pounding.

He made his way down and reunited with Lily.

"Are you okay?" she asked anxiously.

"Fine," he assured her. "Let's get out of here."

As they drove away, the gravity of the situation settled in.

"They're getting desperate," Lily said. "We need to release the story now."

"Agreed," Jake replied. "Let's finish this."

They coordinated with trusted media outlets, ensuring the exposé would be published simultaneously across multiple platforms.

By midday, the story broke—headlines blaring the scandalous details of race fixing and corruption within the racing world.

The reaction was immediate and explosive. Authorities launched investigations, arrests were made, and the sport was thrown into turmoil.

Back at the team's garage, Jake gathered his crew.

"There's something you all need to know," he began, explaining the situation and the revelations.

Shock and disbelief rippled through the team.

"I can't believe it," Sarah said, her voice shaky. "Who would do such a thing?"

Tim shifted uncomfortably, avoiding eye contact.

"Tim," Jake addressed him directly. "Do you have anything to say?"

Tim looked up, guilt etched on his face. "I... I'm sorry," he stammered. "They threatened me. My family..."

Jake's expression softened slightly. "Why didn't you come to us?"

"I was scared," Tim admitted. "They said they'd hurt them if I didn't cooperate."

Emma stepped forward. "We could have helped you."

"I'm so sorry," Tim repeated, tears welling in his eyes.

Jake sighed. "What's done is done. But you need to cooperate with the authorities."

He nodded solemnly. "I will."

As the dust settled, the team began the process of rebuilding trust and moving forward.

Lily's exposé had not only exposed the corruption but also sparked a call for reform within the sport.

Meeting her at the café where it all began, Jake felt a sense of closure.

"You did it," he said, admiration in his tone.

"We did it," she corrected with a smile.

He raised his coffee mug in a toast. "To truth and perseverance."

"To new beginnings," she added, clinking her mug against his.

As they sat together, the future seemed a little brighter—a testament to what could be achieved when standing against injustice.

The road ahead would still have challenges, but with allies

like Lily by his side, Jake was ready to face whatever came next.

Chapter 11: The Crash

The sun hung low over the Silverstone Circuit, casting long shadows across the asphalt as the crowd buzzed with anticipation. It was the midpoint of the season, and tensions were at an all-time high. The grandstands were packed, the air electric with the roar of engines and the scent of burning rubber.

Jake stood in the paddock, adjusting his gloves while surveying the track. His car, *The Phoenix*, gleamed under the bright lights of the pit lane. The team had worked tirelessly to prepare for this race, implementing new strategies and tightening security after recent events.

"How are you feeling?" Emma asked, approaching him with a clipboard in hand.

"Ready," Jake replied, his gaze steady. "We've got a good setup. Today's the day we make our mark."

She offered a reassuring smile. "Just remember, stick to the plan. Don't let anyone force you into mistakes."

"Got it," he nodded.

Across the way, he spotted **Marcus Reed**, a veteran driver with decades of experience and a reputation for mentoring younger racers. Marcus was known for his sportsmanship and had been a consistent presence on the circuit since Jake was a child.

Marcus caught Jake's eye and walked over. "Jake Turner," he greeted warmly. "Looking sharp out there."

"Marcus," Jake smiled. "Always a pleasure. Any sage advice for today's race?"

Marcus chuckled. "Keep your head on straight and trust your instincts. The track may be the same, but every race is different."

"I appreciate that," Jake replied sincerely.

Marcus lowered his voice slightly. "And watch your back. There's been chatter about some aggressive tactics today."

Jake's expression grew serious. "You think something's up?"

"Just a feeling," Marcus admitted. "Stay alert."

"Will do. Thanks for the heads-up."

As Marcus walked away, Jake felt a pang of unease. The events of the past weeks had left him wary, and Marcus's caution only heightened his suspicions.

The call came to line up on the grid. Jake climbed into *The Phoenix*, the cockpit familiar and comforting. The engine purred as he started it, the vibrations coursing through him like adrenaline.

"All systems go," Sarah's voice came through the earpiece. "You've got this, Jake."

"Copy that," he replied.

The cars lined up, engines revving in a mechanical symphony. The lights above the starting line began their countdown sequence. Red... red... red... green!

They were off. Tires screeched as the pack surged forward, jockeying for position into the first corner. Jake held his line, expertly navigating the chaos of the opening laps.

By lap ten, he had settled into a solid third place behind

Adrian Cole and Marcus Reed. The three of them began to pull away from the rest of the field, a trio of skill and determination.

"You're doing great," Emma's voice encouraged. "Maintain your pace."

Jake focused on the track ahead, each turn a calculated maneuver. As they approached a tight chicane, he noticed Adrian's car behaving erratically, swerving slightly.

"Adrian's having control issues," Jake reported.

"Noted," Sarah replied. "Could be an opportunity."

As they entered the straightaway, Adrian's car suddenly lurched, forcing Marcus to swerve to avoid a collision.

"What the hell is he doing?" Jake muttered.

On the next lap, the situation escalated. Adrian's car cut off Marcus aggressively, causing the veteran to brake hard.

"That's dangerous driving," Emma exclaimed. "Be careful, Jake."

"I'm keeping my distance," he assured her.

But Marcus wasn't one to back down. Determined to reclaim his position, he closed the gap on Adrian. The two entered into a high-speed duel, their cars inches apart.

"Something's not right," Jake thought aloud. "This is reckless."

As they approached the notorious Turn 12—a sharp bend with little margin for error—Jake hung back, sensing trouble.

Suddenly, Adrian's car veered sharply, clipping Marcus's front end. Marcus's car spun out of control, skidding off the track at alarming speed.

"Marcus is off!" Jake shouted.

Time seemed to slow as Marcus's car slammed into the barrier, a sickening crunch echoing across the circuit. Debris flew into the air, and a plume of smoke began to rise.

"Red flag! Red flag!" the race officials announced. "All drivers reduce speed and proceed to the pit lane."

Jake's heart pounded in his chest. "Is he okay?" he demanded over the radio.

"Medical teams are on their way," Emma responded, her voice strained.

He pulled into the pit lane, the atmosphere heavy with shock. Other drivers emerged from their cars, concern etched on their faces.

"Did you see what happened?" Sarah asked urgently as Jake climbed out.

"Adrian cut him off," Jake replied angrily. "It looked intentional."

Emma approached, her expression grim. "They're taking Marcus to the medical center. No updates yet."

Jake glanced over at Adrian's pit area. Adrian stood with his team, a stoic expression on his face. Their eyes met briefly, and Jake felt a surge of rage.

"That was no accident," Jake said through clenched teeth.

"Careful," Emma warned. "We don't know all the facts yet."

He took a deep breath, trying to quell his emotions. "I need to find out what's going on."

Minutes turned into an agonizing hour as they awaited news. Finally, the race director gathered the drivers for an announcement.

"Attention, everyone," he began solemnly. "It is with deep regret that we inform you Marcus Reed has succumbed to his injuries."

Gasps and murmurs rippled through the crowd. Jake felt as if the ground had dropped beneath him. Marcus—a legend, a mentor, a friend—was gone.

"This can't be happening," he whispered.

The director continued, "An investigation into the incident is underway. We ask for your cooperation during this difficult time."

As the gathering dispersed, Jake's grief transformed into determination. He approached Adrian, who was surrounded by his team.

"Adrian!" Jake called out sharply.

Adrian turned to face him, his expression unreadable. "Yes?"

"What the hell was that out there?" Jake demanded, his voice low but intense.

"I don't know what you mean," Adrian replied coolly.

"Don't play dumb," Jake snapped. "You drove him off the track."

Adrian narrowed his eyes. "It was a racing incident. Unfortunate, but these things happen."

"Unfortunate?" Jake echoed incredulously. "Marcus is dead!"

A flicker of emotion crossed Adrian's face—was it remorse or something else? "I'm aware," he said quietly. "But accusing me won't change anything."

Before Jake could respond, Victor Reynolds appeared beside Adrian. "Is there a problem here?"

Jake glared at Victor. "Stay out of this."

Victor smirked. "Emotions are running high. Perhaps it's best if we all take some time to cool off."

"You're involved in this, aren't you?" Jake accused. "I won't let you get away with it."

Victor's eyes hardened. "Careful, Turner. Making unfounded allegations can have consequences."

"That's enough," Emma intervened, pulling Jake back. "This isn't the time or place."

Jake allowed himself to be led away, his mind racing. He couldn't shake the feeling that Marcus's death was no mere accident.

Back at their garage, the team gathered in somber silence.

"Marcus was one of the best," Luis said, his voice heavy with sorrow. "He didn't deserve this."

"No, he didn't," Jake agreed. "And I'm going to find out what really happened."

"Jake," Sarah cautioned, "we need to let the officials handle the investigation."

"Do you trust them?" he challenged. "With everything that's been going on?"

She hesitated. "I don't know."

Emma placed a hand on Jake's shoulder. "I understand how you feel, but we need to be smart about this."

He looked at his team—his friends—and made a decision. "I'm going to see Lily. She might be able to help."

Later that evening, Jake met Lily at her apartment. She greeted him with a hug, sensing his distress.

"I'm so sorry about Marcus," she said softly.

"Thanks," he replied, his voice strained. "I need your help. I think his death wasn't an accident."

She led him inside. "Tell me everything."

He recounted the events of the race, the aggressive driving, and Adrian's suspicious behavior.

"Lily, I know you've been digging into the race fixing and the network behind it. Is it possible this is connected?"

She considered his words. "It's possible. Marcus was known for his integrity. If he got wind of their operations, they might have seen him as a threat."

"Can you look into it?" Jake asked urgently. "We need evidence."

"I'll do everything I can," she promised. "But we have to be cautious. They're becoming more dangerous."

He nodded, the weight of grief and anger pressing down on him. "I can't let Marcus's death be in vain."

She squeezed his hand reassuringly. "We'll get to the bottom of this together."

Over the next few days, Lily dove into her investigation, utilizing her contacts and resources to uncover any information related to the crash. Jake focused on the technical aspects, reviewing footage and telemetry data from the race.

In the team's workshop, Sarah and Luis assisted Jake in analyzing the data.

"Look at this," Sarah pointed to a spike in the telemetry. "Adrian's car made an unusual maneuver right before the collision."

"Can we prove it was intentional?" Jake asked.

"It's not definitive," Luis admitted. "But it's suspicious."

Emma joined them. "I've been hearing rumors that Adrian's team made last-minute modifications to his car."

"What kind of modifications?" Jake inquired.

"Unknown, but if they altered the steering or braking systems, it could explain his erratic driving."

Jake's jaw tightened. "We need to get access to his car's data."

"That's going to be nearly impossible," Sarah cautioned. "They'll guard that information closely."

"Maybe not," Emma interjected thoughtfully. "I might know someone who can help."

That evening, Emma arranged a meeting with **David Patel**, a former engineer for Adrian's team who had left under contentious circumstances.

They met at a discreet location—a quiet bar away from the usual racing haunts.

"David, thank you for meeting us," Emma greeted him.

"Anything for an old friend," he replied, though his demeanor was wary. "What do you need?"

"We're investigating the crash that killed Marcus Reed," Jake explained. "We believe Adrian's car may have been tampered with."

David sighed. "I heard about Marcus. Terrible tragedy."

"Do you know if Adrian's team made any unusual modifications before the race?" Emma asked.

He hesitated, glancing around before lowering his voice. "I shouldn't be telling you this, but yes. They've been experimenting with a new active steering system."

"Active steering?" Jake repeated. "That could override driver input."

"Exactly," David confirmed. "It's controlled remotely to make micro-adjustments. Highly illegal under racing regulations."

"Do you have proof?" Emma pressed.

He nodded reluctantly. "I kept copies of the development logs and schematics as insurance. I can get them to you."

"Thank you," Jake said earnestly. "This could change everything."

"Be careful," David warned. "If they find out I'm helping you, it won't end well."

"We'll protect your identity," Emma assured him.

With the new evidence in hand, Jake and his team compiled a comprehensive report. Lily added her findings, including communications that suggested Victor Reynolds had orchestrated the use of the active steering system to manipulate race outcomes.

They presented their case to the racing commission, demanding a thorough investigation.

"This is serious," the lead official acknowledged, reviewing the documents. "We'll need to impound Adrian's car and conduct an independent analysis."

Word spread quickly, and the media swarmed the circuit. Adrian vehemently denied the allegations in press conferences, calling them baseless attacks on his character.

Victor Reynolds remained elusive, issuing a generic statement of support for the investigation while distancing himself from any wrongdoing.

As the investigation unfolded, tensions escalated. Jake received anonymous threats urging him to drop the matter.

One evening, his car was vandalized—tires slashed, windows shattered.

"That's it," Jake declared to his team. "They're trying to intimidate us, but we won't back down."

"Agreed," Emma said firmly. "We stand together."

Lily reported the incident to the authorities, who increased security around the team.

The investigation reached its climax when the commission announced their findings: evidence confirmed that Adrian's car had been fitted with the illegal active steering system. Furthermore, data logs showed that the system had been activated during the race, leading directly to the collision with Marcus Reed.

Adrian was suspended pending further disciplinary action. Victor Reynolds was implicated as the mastermind behind the scheme, facing criminal charges for conspiracy and manslaughter.

Justice, it seemed, was finally being served.

At a memorial service for Marcus, the racing community gathered to honor his legacy. Stories were shared of his generosity, mentorship, and passion for the sport.

Jake stood before the assembled crowd, delivering a heartfelt eulogy.

"Marcus was more than a competitor," he said, his voice steady despite the emotion welling inside. "He was a mentor, a friend, and an inspiration to us all. He stood for integrity, for fairness, and for the pure love of racing. We owe it to him to carry on those values."

After the service, Jake found a quiet spot overlooking the track. Lily joined him, the two standing in contemplative silence.

"He would be proud of you," she said softly.

"I hope so," Jake replied. "It's bittersweet. We exposed the corruption, but at such a cost."

She touched his arm gently. "Sometimes doing the right thing comes with sacrifice. But because of you, the sport can begin to heal."

He nodded, taking comfort in her words. "Thank you for being by my side through all of this."

"Always," she smiled.

As the sun set, casting a golden glow over the empty stands, Jake felt a renewed sense of purpose. There was still much to do—rebuilding trust, continuing the fight for integrity—but he was not alone.

"Ready to get back on the track?" Lily asked.

"More than ever," he affirmed. "For Marcus, for the team, for everyone who believes in what racing should be."

They walked away together, the echoes of engines and cheers a distant memory, but the promise of a new beginning shining ahead.

Chapter 12: Echoes of Danger

The roar of engines faded as the sun dipped below the horizon, casting long shadows across the deserted racetrack. The day's practice sessions had concluded, and the once-bustling paddock was now eerily quiet. Jake lingered by *The Phoenix*, his fingers tracing the sleek lines of the car. The events of recent weeks weighed heavily on him—the loss of Marcus Reed, the exposure of corruption, and the unsettling feeling that the battle was far from over.

"Hey, Jake," Emma's voice called out, breaking the silence. She approached with a concerned expression. "You okay? You've been out here a while."

He offered a faint smile. "Just thinking. It's been a lot to process."

She nodded, her gaze sympathetic. "I understand. The whole team is feeling it. But we need you sharp."

"I know," he sighed. "I won't let it distract me."

As they walked back toward the garage, the distant hum of generators filled the air. The rest of the team had already left, leaving the facility bathed in the glow of security lights.

"Did you see Lily today?" Emma asked.

"She's following up on some leads," Jake replied. "Still digging into Victor Reynolds's network."

Emma frowned. "Even after his arrest, there's more to uncover?"

"Apparently. She thinks there are still people pulling strings behind the scenes."

They reached the garage, and Jake locked up, securing *The Phoenix* for the night.

"Get some rest," Emma advised. "Tomorrow's another big day."

"Will do," he assured her. "Good night."

As he headed to the parking lot, a cool breeze rustled through the trees lining the path. The scent of fresh rain lingered in the air—a brief afternoon shower had left the ground damp, puddles reflecting the pale moonlight.

Jake unlocked his car and slid into the driver's seat. As he started the engine, his phone buzzed with a new message. Glancing at the screen, he saw an unknown number.

Unknown: You should have walked away when you had the chance.

A chill ran down his spine. He typed a quick reply.

Jake: Who is this?

Almost immediately, a response appeared.

Unknown: A final warning. Back off, or you'll regret it.

He stared at the message, a knot forming in his stomach. Was this a prank? Or something more sinister?

Determined not to be intimidated, he drove home, but the unease lingered. Upon arriving at his apartment building, he noticed a black sedan parked across the street. Its windows were tinted, concealing the occupants. Jake hesitated before pulling into his usual spot, his senses on high alert.

As he exited his car, the sedan's engine roared to life, and it sped away into the night.

"Paranoid," he muttered to himself, shaking off the discomfort. "It's just a coincidence."

Entering his apartment, he double-checked the locks before tossing his keys onto the kitchen counter. The city lights twinkled outside his window, but tonight they offered little comfort.

His phone buzzed again. Another message from the unknown number.

Unknown: You're being watched. Next time, we won't be so subtle.

Anger flared within him. He dialed the number, but it went straight to voicemail. Frustrated, he left a message.

"Listen, whoever you are, I'm not backing down. If you have a problem, say it to my face."

He hung up, his heart pounding. Deciding he needed backup, he called Lily.

"Jake?" she answered, concern evident in her voice. "It's late. Everything okay?"

"I've been getting threats," he explained. "Anonymous messages telling me to back off."

She paused. "I was afraid this might happen. You're rattling cages, Jake. They see you as a threat."

"Who are 'they'?" he demanded. "Victor's behind bars."

"Yes, but his associates aren't," she cautioned. "There are still players in this game who want to keep their operations running."

He rubbed his temples. "What should I do?"

"First, don't engage with them," she advised. "Save all the messages. We can report them to the authorities."

"I saw a suspicious car outside my place tonight," he added. "Think I'm being followed."

"Stay vigilant," she urged. "Maybe stay somewhere else for a few days."

"I can't live in fear," he protested.

"You're not—you're being smart," she countered. "Let me make some calls. We'll figure this out."

"Alright," he conceded. "Thanks, Lily."

"Anytime. Keep your doors locked."

After hanging up, Jake secured all the windows and drew the curtains. Sleep was elusive that night, his mind racing with possibilities. Shadows seemed to move in the corners of his vision, every creak of the building amplified in the silence.

The next morning, fatigue clung to him as he arrived at the racetrack. The team noticed his haggard appearance.

"Rough night?" Sarah asked gently.

"Didn't sleep well," he admitted.

"Everything okay?" Luis inquired.

"Just some personal stuff," Jake deflected. "Nothing to worry about."

Emma pulled him aside. "I can tell something's up. Talk to me."

He sighed, debating whether to share his concerns. Finally, he relented. "I've been getting anonymous threats. Telling me to back off racing and stop digging into the corruption."

Her eyes widened. "Jake, that's serious. Why didn't you tell us sooner?"

"I didn't want to alarm anyone," he replied. "But Lily thinks it's connected to Victor's associates."

"We need to inform the authorities," she insisted. "And maybe beef up security."

"I agree," he nodded. "I'll handle it today."

Practice sessions began, and Jake tried to focus on the track. The familiar rhythm of driving usually brought him peace, but today, distractions plagued him. Every glance at the stands made him wonder if someone was watching, waiting.

Midway through the session, his radio crackled. "Jake, everything alright?" Emma's voice asked.

"Yeah," he lied. "Just a bit off my game."

"Bring it in for a pit stop," she suggested.

He pulled into the pit lane, and the team swarmed the car.

"Nothing wrong mechanically," Sarah reported after a quick check.

"Maybe take a short break," Emma advised.

He climbed out of the car, removing his helmet. "Maybe that's a good idea."

As he walked toward the team lounge, a track official approached him.

"Mr. Turner?"

"Yes?"

"This was left for you at the front gate." The official handed him a small envelope.

Jake's name was scrawled on the front in block letters. He hesitated before opening it. Inside was a single sheet of paper with a typed message.

Last chance. Withdraw from the next race, or face the consequences.

His jaw tightened. "Did you see who left this?" he asked the official.

"Sorry, sir. It was found on the ground near the gate."

"Thanks," Jake muttered, dismissing him.

He showed the note to Emma. "They're escalating."

Her expression hardened. "This can't continue. We need to take action."

"I'll report it to the race authorities and the police," he agreed. "But I'm not backing down."

"Let's also review our security footage," she suggested. "Maybe we can spot something."

They spent the next hour combing through camera feeds.

Near the front gate, a figure in a hooded jacket appeared briefly, dropping the envelope before slipping away.

"Can we enhance the image?" Jake asked.

"I'll try," Sarah said, working her technical magic. The image sharpened slightly, but the person's face remained obscured.

"Whoever it is knows how to avoid cameras," Luis commented.

"Or they have inside knowledge," Jake added grimly.

An uneasy silence settled over the group.

"You think someone on the team is involved?" Sarah asked cautiously.

"It's a possibility," Emma acknowledged. "But we can't jump to conclusions."

"Trust has to be earned," Jake said. "Especially now."

They decided to limit access to sensitive areas and information, tightening their internal security.

As the day progressed, Jake couldn't shake the feeling of being watched. During a break, he stepped outside for some air, only to notice the same black sedan from the previous night parked near the perimeter fence.

His phone buzzed with a new message.

Unknown: Nice car. Shame if something happened to it.

He snapped a photo of the sedan and the message, forwarding both to Lily and the authorities.

"Enough is enough," he muttered.

Returning to the garage, he found a small crowd gathered around *The Phoenix*.

"What's going on?" he called out.

Max turned to him, concern etched on his face. "Someone tampered with your car."

Jake's heart sank. "What?"

"Sarah noticed the fuel panel was slightly ajar," Max explained. "We checked and found traces of sugar in the fuel tank."

"Sabotage," Jake spat. "Did anyone see anything?"

"Not yet," Max replied. "We're reviewing the footage."

Anger simmered within Jake. "They're trying to take me out—literally."

Emma placed a hand on his shoulder. "We'll get to the bottom of this. But you need to stay safe."

"Maybe you should lay low for a while," Max suggested reluctantly.

"No," Jake insisted. "That's exactly what they want. I'm not giving them the satisfaction."

"At least let us increase security around you," Emma urged.

"Fine," he conceded. "But I'm not backing down from the race."

They doubled their efforts, implementing stricter protocols

and hiring additional security personnel.

Later that evening, Jake met with Detective Laura Mitchell, the officer assigned to his case.

"Mr. Turner, we've reviewed the threats you've received," she began. "We're taking this seriously."

"Do you have any leads?" he asked.

"We're analyzing the messages and the photos you provided," she said. "The vehicle you mentioned is registered to a shell company tied to Victor Reynolds's associates."

"So they are still active," Jake surmised.

"It appears so," she confirmed. "We're keeping an eye on known affiliates. In the meantime, I recommend being cautious."

"Believe me, I am."

"If you receive any more threats or notice anything unusual, contact me immediately," she instructed.

"Will do," he agreed.

Leaving the police station, Jake felt a mix of frustration and resolve. The shadows of danger were closing in, but he refused to be intimidated.

His phone rang—Lily.

"Hey, any news?" he answered.

"I dug up some information," she said. "There's a figure known as 'The Broker' who's been coordinating activities since Victor's arrest."

"The Broker?" Jake repeated. "Sounds ominous."

"He's elusive," Lily explained. "But I have a contact who might know more."

"Is it safe?"

"I'll be careful," she assured him. "We need to expose whoever is behind this."

"Agreed," he said. "Keep me posted."

"Stay safe, Jake."

"You too."

The next morning, Jake arrived at the track to find a police car parked outside the garage.

"Detective Mitchell?" he greeted as she approached.

"Mr. Turner, we received a tip overnight," she informed him. "There was chatter about an attempt on your life."

His eyes widened. "When?"

"Possibly during the upcoming race."

Emma joined them, overhearing the conversation. "What's going on?"

"There's a credible threat," the detective stated. "We recommend withdrawing from the race until we can ensure your safety."

Jake bristled. "I can't do that. If I back out, they win."

"Your life is more important than a race," Emma argued.

"I appreciate the concern," he said firmly. "But I won't let them control me through fear."

Detective Mitchell sighed. "In that case, we'll have officers stationed throughout the venue. We'll also have plainclothes agents in the crowd."

"Thank you," Jake replied.

As preparations for the race continued, the atmosphere was tense. The team worked diligently, but an undercurrent of anxiety permeated the air.

Lily arrived, her expression serious. "I have news," she announced quietly.

They gathered in a secluded area.

"I found out that 'The Broker' is planning something big," she revealed. "He's been hiring mercenaries—dangerous people."

"Do you know what they're planning?" Jake asked.

"Not exactly, but it's centered around the race," she said. "They might attempt to sabotage your car during the event, or worse."

Emma looked alarmed. "Jake, this is escalating beyond what we can handle."

He considered their words, a storm of emotions swirling within him. "I can't walk away," he declared. "If I do, they'll just target someone else."

"Then we need a plan," Lily asserted. "We can set a trap, expose them."

"How?" he inquired.

"By anticipating their move," she explained. "We work with the authorities to catch them in the act."

He glanced at Emma. "Are you with me?"

She met his gaze unwaveringly. "All the way."

They coordinated with Detective Mitchell, devising a strategy to lure out the perpetrators while ensuring Jake's safety.

Race day arrived, the grandstands filled with eager spectators unaware of the underlying danger. Security was tight, officers strategically placed throughout the facility.

Jake suited up, his mind focused. "Let's do this," he told his team.

"Be careful out there," Emma urged.

"Always," he assured her.

As the race commenced, Jake maintained a steady pace, his senses attuned to any irregularities. Halfway through, he noticed a car tailing him aggressively—one he didn't recognize.

"Emma, who's car 27?" he asked over the radio.

She checked the roster. "There is no car 27 registered."

Alarm bells rang in his mind. "I think we found our threat."

"Authorities are alerted," she responded. "Stay sharp."

The rogue car accelerated, attempting to force him off the track. Jake maneuvered skillfully, avoiding collisions while signaling to officials.

Suddenly, the car drew alongside him, and he caught a glimpse of the driver's cold, determined eyes. The driver swerved, sideswiping *The Phoenix*.

"Hang on, Jake!" Emma's voice was tense.

He fought for control, gripping the wheel tightly. The rogue driver prepared for another hit, but before he could act, police vehicles appeared along the track perimeter, lights flashing.

"Backup is here," Emma informed him.

The driver hesitated, realizing the net was closing in. In a desperate move, he accelerated toward the pit lane, but was intercepted by security personnel.

Jake breathed a sigh of relief. "They got him."

"Race control is calling a safety car," Emma said. "Return to the pit lane."

He complied, pulling in as the crowd buzzed with confusion over the sudden interruption.

Detective Mitchell met him as he exited the car. "Good work, Jake. We apprehended the suspect."

"Who is he?" Jake asked.

"A hired mercenary," she revealed. "And we found communications linking him to 'The Broker.'"

Lily joined them, a triumphant smile on her face. "We did it. We have enough evidence to bring them down."

"Thanks to you both," Jake said gratefully.

Emma approached, relief evident. "I'm glad you're okay."

He smiled. "Couldn't have done it without all of you."

In the aftermath, authorities conducted raids based on the information gathered, dismantling the remnants of Victor Reynolds's network. 'The Broker' was identified and arrested, his operations exposed.

The racing community rallied around Jake, praising his courage and resilience. Safety protocols were enhanced, and a renewed commitment to integrity permeated the sport.

At a press conference, Jake addressed the media.

"I stand here today not just as a driver, but as someone who believes in the true spirit of racing," he declared. "We faced adversity, but together we overcame it. I want to thank my team, the authorities, and everyone who supported us."

As he stepped away from the podium, Lily and Emma greeted him with proud smiles.

"You handled that well," Lily complimented.

"Thanks," he replied. "But I couldn't have done any of this without you both."

"What's next?" Emma asked.

He grinned. "Back to what we love—racing."

They walked toward the paddock, the sun shining brightly overhead. The shadows of danger had receded, replaced by hope and camaraderie.

For Jake, the echoes of the past served as a reminder of the challenges he had overcome and the strength he had found within himself and his allies.

The road ahead was open, and he was ready to embrace it.

Chapter 13: Under Pressure

The afternoon sun beat down on the racetrack, casting shimmering heat waves off the asphalt. Jake sat in the team's trailer, a cold bottle of water in hand, as he waited for his next meeting. The practice session had gone well, but his mind was elsewhere. The recent threats and attempts on his life had taken a toll, but today, his concerns were shifting to another pressing matter: funding.

Emma entered the trailer, a stack of folders tucked under her arm. "They're ready for you," she said softly.

Jake nodded, rising from his seat. "How do they seem?"

"Impatient," she admitted. "But we can handle this."

He took a deep breath. "Let's get it over with."

They made their way to the conference room where representatives from their primary sponsors—**Titan Dynamics** and **Velocity Corp**—were waiting. The atmosphere was tense, the air thick with unspoken expectations.

"Jake, Emma," greeted **Robert Lang**, the stern-faced executive from Titan Dynamics. His counterpart from Velocity Corp, **Susan Hartley**, offered a curt nod.

"Thank you for meeting with us," Jake began, trying to project confidence.

"Let's cut to the chase," Robert said, folding his hands on the table. "Your recent performance has been... underwhelming."

Jake exchanged a quick glance with Emma. "We've faced

some challenges, but we're overcoming them," he replied.

"Challenges are part of racing," Susan interjected. "But our investment demands results."

Emma leaned forward. "With all due respect, we've made significant progress in improving the car's performance. Jake's skill on the track is undeniable."

Robert raised an eyebrow. "Skill isn't the issue. It's about winning. Podium finishes generate exposure, and exposure drives sales. Without that, our partnership becomes less... beneficial."

Jake felt a surge of frustration. "I've been dealing with serious threats to my safety. Sabotage attempts, harassment—you name it. We're handling more than just competition on the track."

Susan sighed. "We're aware of the incidents, but our board isn't interested in excuses. They want assurance that their investment is yielding returns."

"Are you saying you're considering pulling our funding?" Emma asked sharply.

Robert exchanged a glance with Susan before responding. "Not yet. But we're evaluating all options. Other drivers and teams are eager for opportunities."

Jake's jaw tightened. "I've given everything to this sport and to our sponsors. We've been fighting not just to win races but to preserve the integrity of racing itself."

"Integrity doesn't pay the bills," Susan said bluntly.

Emma placed a hand on Jake's arm, a subtle reminder to stay composed. "What can we do to assure you that we're committed to success?"

Robert leaned back in his chair. "Win the next race. Show us that you can deliver under pressure."

"And if we don't?" Jake challenged.

"Then we'll have to reconsider our partnership," Susan stated.

The ultimatum hung heavy in the air. Jake took a moment before responding. "Understood. We'll give you the results you're looking for."

The sponsors stood, signaling the end of the meeting. "We look forward to seeing your performance," Robert said before exiting with Susan.

Once they were gone, Jake exhaled deeply. "They're squeezing us."

Emma nodded. "They're not giving us much room to breathe."

"I can't shake the feeling that there's more to this," Jake mused. "Their timing, the pressure—it's all too coincidental."

"You think they're involved in the larger scheme?" Emma asked quietly.

"It's possible," he admitted. "We know that some sponsors have ties to the corruption we've been fighting against. They might be trying to manipulate us."

Emma considered this. "We need to tread carefully. If they're connected, pushing back could make us more of a target."

"Agreed," Jake said. "But we can't let them control us."

They spent the next few hours strategizing, reviewing race data, and refining their approach. The upcoming race would be critical—not just for their standing but for their future as a team.

Later that evening, Jake met with Lily at a quiet café.

"I heard about the sponsor meeting," she said sympathetically.

"News travels fast," he remarked wryly.

"One of my contacts at the circuit mentioned it," she explained. "How are you holding up?"

"Frustrated," he admitted. "They're giving us an ultimatum: win or lose funding."

She stirred her tea thoughtfully. "That puts a lot of pressure on you."

"Exactly what they want," Jake said. "I suspect they might be tied to the corruption. Maybe they're trying to push me into making mistakes."

Lily's eyes narrowed. "I wouldn't be surprised. I've been digging into Titan Dynamics and Velocity Corp. There are some questionable transactions that link them to shell companies associated with Victor Reynolds's network."

"So they could be part of the bigger picture," Jake concluded.

"Potentially," she confirmed. "But I need more evidence."

"Meanwhile, I have to race like everything's normal," he sighed.

She reached across the table, her hand brushing his. "You're not alone in this. We'll find a way to expose them."

He offered a grateful smile. "Thank you, Lily."

As they parted ways, Jake felt a renewed sense of determination. If his sponsors were indeed part of the corruption, he would need to outsmart them at their own game.

Back at his apartment, he reviewed footage from previous races, looking for any signs of manipulation or interference. Hours passed as he analyzed every detail, his mind focused on uncovering the truth.

The next morning, he shared his findings with Emma and the team.

"Look at this," he pointed to a moment in a recent race. "Our telemetry data shows a sudden drop in power, but there's no mechanical reason for it."

Sarah examined the data. "You're right. It's as if something interfered electronically."

"Could someone have hacked into our systems?" Luis speculated.

"It's possible," Emma agreed. "If our sponsors are involved, they might have access to our technical data."

Jake clenched his fists. "They're sabotaging us to ensure we underperform, then threatening to pull funding when we don't meet expectations."

"We need to secure our systems," Sarah declared. "I'll implement new encryption protocols and firewalls."

"Good," Jake said. "But we also need to gather evidence of

their interference."

Emma nodded. "I'll monitor communications and look for any unauthorized access attempts."

As the team mobilized, Jake felt a surge of camaraderie. They were in this together, and they wouldn't go down without a fight.

On the day of the race, the atmosphere was tense. The grandstands were filled with spectators, the air buzzing with anticipation.

Jake suited up, his helmet under his arm as he approached *The Phoenix*. Emma stood beside him, her expression resolute.

"We've got this," she assured him.

He nodded. "No matter what happens, we do this our way."

As he climbed into the cockpit, Sarah's voice came over the radio. "All systems are secure. No signs of interference."

"Thanks, Sarah," he replied. "Let's make this one count."

The race began, and Jake drove with a focused intensity. Each lap was a calculated maneuver, his skill and precision pushing him ahead of the competition.

Midway through the race, an unexpected development occurred. A rival driver, sponsored by Velocity Corp, began tailing him aggressively.

"Watch out for car number 22," Emma warned. "He's making risky moves."

"I see him," Jake acknowledged.

The driver attempted to force Jake into errors, but Jake anticipated each tactic, maintaining his lead.

As the final laps approached, Jake felt a surge of adrenaline. Victory was within reach.

Suddenly, his radio crackled with interference. "—ake, do you copy?"

"Emma? You're breaking up," he replied.

Static filled his earpiece, followed by a distorted voice he didn't recognize. "Back off, or face the consequences."

His heart raced. They were trying to distract him.

"Not this time," he muttered.

He focused on the track, blocking out the noise. With a final burst of speed, he crossed the finish line first, the crowd erupting in cheers.

"Yes!" Emma's voice came through clearly now. "You did it!"

Relief and triumph washed over him. "We did it," he corrected.

In the winner's circle, Jake accepted the trophy, his smile masking the turmoil within. As he glanced toward the sponsors' suite, he saw Robert Lang and Susan Hartley watching impassively.

Back in the team's garage, celebrations were in full swing.

"That was incredible!" Luis exclaimed.

"Way to show them," Sarah added.

Emma approached, her eyes shining. "Proud of you, Jake."

"Thanks," he said sincerely. "But we still have work to do."

Lily arrived, weaving through the crowd. "Congratulations," she said, hugging him.

"Glad you could make it," he replied.

She lowered her voice. "I have news. I found a connection between our sponsors and the sabotage attempts. They were funding operations to manipulate race outcomes."

Jake's expression hardened. "Then it's time to confront them."

Chapter 14: Old Allies

Later that evening, Jake sat in a dimly lit bar on the outskirts of town, nursing a glass of whiskey. The victory felt hollow knowing that the people who were supposed to support him were working against him.

The door swung open, and a tall figure entered—a man in his late forties with a rugged demeanor and a confident stride. His piercing green eyes scanned the room before settling on Jake.

"Jake Turner?" the man asked as he approached.

Jake looked up, curiosity piqued. "That's me."

The man extended a hand. "Name's **Alex Mercer**. I hear you're looking for information about the darker side of racing."

Jake shook his hand. "Depends on who's asking."

Alex chuckled, taking a seat across from him. "Fair enough. I was a driver once, like you. Retired now, but I still keep an ear to the ground."

"Lily mentioned you might be able to help," Jake said cautiously.

"She's a good kid," Alex remarked. "Smart, tenacious. Reminds me of myself in my younger days."

"So, what brings you here?" Jake inquired.

"I heard about your situation," Alex began. "Corrupt sponsors, sabotage, threats—I've seen it all before."

Jake leaned forward. "You have information?"

Alex nodded. "I was in deep with these types back in the day. Got out before it consumed me, but not without learning a few secrets."

"Why help me?" Jake asked.

"Because I believe in the sport," Alex replied earnestly. "Racing used to be about passion and skill. Now, it's tainted by greed and manipulation. If I can help set things right, then maybe it's worth it."

Jake considered his words. "What can you tell me?"

Alex took a sip of his drink. "Your sponsors, Titan Dynamics and Velocity Corp, are more than just backers. They're part of a syndicate that profits from controlling race outcomes. They place bets, manipulate results, and eliminate obstacles."

"Obstacles like me," Jake said grimly.

"Exactly," Alex confirmed. "They pressure drivers to comply. Those who resist face consequences—career sabotage, or worse."

"Do you have proof?" Jake pressed.

"I've kept records," Alex revealed. "Documents, recordings, names of key players. It's risky, but with the right exposure, we can bring them down."

Jake felt a surge of hope. "This could change everything."

"But we need to be careful," Alex warned. "They're powerful and won't hesitate to silence us."

"I'm aware," Jake acknowledged. "They've already tried."

Alex studied him for a moment. "You've got guts, kid. Reminds me of myself."

"Then let's use that to our advantage," Jake proposed. "Work together to expose them."

Alex extended his hand again. "Agreed."

They spent the next several hours going over the evidence Alex had gathered. The information was damning—financial records showing bribes, communication logs detailing race manipulation plans, and connections to illegal betting rings.

"This is more extensive than I imagined," Jake remarked, scrolling through the files on Alex's laptop.

"They've been operating for years," Alex explained. "Flying under the radar, protected by layers of legitimate business fronts."

"We need to get this to Lily," Jake said. "She can help disseminate it."

"Agreed," Alex replied. "But we have to act fast. Once they realize we're onto them, they'll come after us."

Jake's phone buzzed with a message from Lily.

Lily: Any progress?

He quickly responded.

Jake: Met with Alex Mercer. Have substantial evidence. Let's meet tomorrow to plan next steps.

She replied promptly.

Lily: Great news. Be careful.

As they wrapped up their meeting, Alex offered a word of caution. "Trust is scarce in this business. Be sure of your allies."

"I trust my team," Jake affirmed. "And I trust Lily."

"Good," Alex said. "We'll need all the support we can get."

The following day, Jake, Emma, Lily, and Alex gathered in a secure location—an unused warehouse away from prying eyes.

Lily spread out the documents on a large table. "This is incredible," she said, her eyes scanning the pages. "It's enough to implicate them in multiple crimes."

Emma pointed to a list of names. "These are high-profile individuals. Exposing them will cause a major upheaval."

"Which is exactly what we need," Jake asserted. "To root out the corruption."

Alex leaned against a pillar. "We need to ensure this information reaches the right channels. The authorities, reputable media outlets—anywhere it can't be suppressed."

Lily nodded. "I have contacts who can help. But we also need to protect ourselves."

"Agreed," Emma said. "They won't go down without a fight."

As they strategized, a sense of unity formed among them. They were a small group against a formidable enemy, but their shared goal strengthened their resolve.

"There's one more thing," Alex mentioned. "They have a meeting scheduled tomorrow night—a gathering of key members of the syndicate. If we can get recordings or evidence from that meeting, it would seal the case."

"How do we get in?" Jake asked.

"I still have connections," Alex revealed. "I can secure an invitation for one or two of us."

"It's too dangerous," Emma cautioned.

"I'll go," Jake volunteered. "They already know me."

"I don't like it," Emma objected. "You're putting yourself at risk."

"It's a risk I'm willing to take," he insisted.

Lily interjected. "If Jake goes, he'll need backup. I'll be nearby, monitoring communications."

"Alright," Alex agreed. "But we need to prepare."

The next evening, Jake arrived at the opulent mansion where the meeting was to take place. Dressed in a sharp suit, he blended in with the affluent guests milling about the grand foyer.

Alex had provided him with a discreet recording device and a communication earpiece linked to Lily.

"Remember," Alex had advised, "act natural. They're expecting you to be curious about their operations."

"Got it," Jake had replied.

As he navigated through the crowd, he spotted familiar faces—executives, team owners, and other influential figures.

Robert Lang approached him, a sly smile on his face. "Jake Turner, what a surprise."

"Robert," Jake greeted coolly. "I was invited. Thought it might be an opportunity to discuss our partnership."

"Indeed," Robert replied. "Come, join us."

He led Jake to a private room where a group had assembled, including Susan Hartley and other syndicate members.

"Glad you could make it," Susan said, her tone dripping with false warmth.

Jake maintained his composure. "Always interested in opportunities."

Robert raised a glass. "To mutually beneficial arrangements."

The group echoed the toast, sipping their drinks.

"As you know, we're invested in more than just racing," Robert began. "We're shaping the future of the sport."

"By any means necessary," Susan added with a pointed look.

Jake feigned interest. "I'm listening."

They began discussing plans to expand their influence, mentioning bribes to officials, manipulation of regulations, and control over race outcomes.

Jake's recording device captured every word.

"You've proven to be a valuable asset," Robert told him. "With your cooperation, we can ensure your continued success."

"And if I choose not to cooperate?" Jake challenged lightly.

Susan's eyes hardened. "That wouldn't be wise."

Robert placed a hand on Jake's shoulder. "Think of the possibilities, Jake. Wealth, fame, power—all within your grasp."

He forced a smile. "It's an intriguing proposition."

"Excellent," Robert said. "We'll discuss details soon."

As the meeting concluded, Jake excused himself, making his way toward the exit.

"Did you get everything?" Lily's voice sounded in his earpiece.

"Yes," he whispered. "Heading out now."

He reached the front door when a security guard stepped in front of him. "Leaving so soon?"

"Yes, early day tomorrow," Jake replied smoothly.

The guard eyed him suspiciously but stepped aside. "Have a good night."

Relieved, Jake exited the mansion and headed toward his car. Suddenly, he heard footsteps behind him.

"Going somewhere?" a voice sneered.

He turned to see two men approaching, their intentions clear.

"Just heading home," Jake said calmly.

"Not before we have a chat," one of them said, reaching for him.

Before they could act, a car screeched to a halt nearby. The door flew open, and Alex shouted, "Get in!"

Jake sprinted to the car, diving inside as Alex hit the gas. The men shouted after them, but it was too late.

"Cutting it close," Jake remarked, catching his breath.

"Thought you might need a ride," Alex replied with a grin.

"Thanks," Jake said sincerely.

They rendezvoused with Emma and Lily at a safe location.

"That was too close," Emma scolded, relief evident in her eyes.

"But we got what we needed," Jake said, holding up the recording device.

Lily connected it to her laptop, playing back the incriminating conversation.

"This is more than enough," she declared. "We'll send copies to law enforcement and major news outlets."

"Let's make sure it can't be suppressed," Alex advised.

They spent the night distributing the evidence, covering all bases to ensure the information went public.

By morning, headlines blared:

"Major Racing Syndicate Exposed: Corruption at the Highest Levels"

Arrests were made swiftly. Robert Lang, Susan Hartley, and other key figures were taken into custody. The racing world was thrown into upheaval, but a sense of justice prevailed.

Jake's sponsors were terminated, but new offers poured in from reputable companies eager to associate with his integrity and courage.

At a press conference, Jake addressed the media.

"I stand here today proud of what we've accomplished," he said. "Not just as a team, but as a community committed to preserving the true spirit of racing. We faced adversity, but we didn't back down. This sport belongs to all of us who love it honestly and passionately."

The crowd applauded, admiration evident.

Afterward, Jake joined Emma, Lily, and Alex backstage.

"You did it," Emma said, hugging him.

"We did it," he corrected, smiling at each of them.

Alex extended his hand. "Proud of you, Jake. You're the kind of driver this sport needs."

"Thank you for everything," Jake replied, shaking his hand firmly.

Lily's eyes shone with emotion. "So, what's next for Jake Turner?"

He grinned. "Back to the track, of course. And maybe a little less drama."

They laughed, the tension of the past weeks finally lifting.

As they walked away, the sun setting in the distance, Jake felt a profound sense of accomplishment. The road ahead was uncertain, but with loyal allies and a renewed commitment to integrity, he was ready to face whatever challenges came his way.

Chapter 15: High Stakes

The sun dipped low over the Monaco harbor, casting a golden glow on the yachts bobbing gently in the water. The Grand Prix was just days away, and the city buzzed with anticipation. For Jake Turner, however, the glamour of Monte Carlo was overshadowed by a lingering sense of unease.

Sitting on the balcony of his hotel room, Jake gazed out at the shimmering Mediterranean Sea. His thoughts were interrupted by a knock at the door. He opened it to find Lily, her expression serious.

"Mind if I come in?" she asked.

"Of course," Jake replied, stepping aside. "What's going on?"

Lily entered, clutching a folder tightly to her chest. "I have some information you need to see."

They settled at a small table. Lily spread out documents and photographs, her eyes meeting his. "I've uncovered an illegal betting ring operating within the racing circuit," she began. "It's extensive, and it involves some high-profile figures."

Jake leaned forward, scanning the materials. "Who are we talking about?"

"Team owners, sponsors, even some race officials," she revealed. "They're manipulating race outcomes to maximize their profits."

He shook his head in disbelief. "I thought we dismantled the major corruption rings."

"This is different," she explained. "They've been operating in the shadows, adapting after we exposed the previous syndicate."

Jake's gaze hardened. "Do they have ties to our team?"

Lily hesitated. "I haven't found any direct links to your current team members, but... there's something else." She handed him a photograph of **Richard Stanton**, the influential head of the International Racing Federation.

"Stanton?" Jake exclaimed. "He's involved?"

"It appears so," Lily confirmed. "He's been using his position to cover up their activities and ensure certain drivers succeed or fail based on the bets placed."

A knot formed in Jake's stomach. "This changes everything. If Stanton is involved, the entire sport is compromised."

"There's more," Lily continued. "I intercepted communications indicating that they're targeting you specifically. Your success has been unpredictable, making it harder for them to control outcomes."

Jake sat back, absorbing the weight of her words. "So they're planning to sabotage me?"

"Or worse," she warned. "We need to be cautious."

He rubbed his temples. "We can't let this continue. But taking on Stanton and his network won't be easy."

"I've already started gathering evidence," Lily said. "But we'll need solid proof to bring them down."

Just then, Jake's phone buzzed with a message from an unknown number.

Unknown: Be careful where you tread. Some paths lead to dangerous ends.

He showed the message to Lily. "They're watching me."

She frowned. "We need to act fast."

The next day, Jake met with his team in a private conference room at the paddock. Emma, Sarah, Luis, and Alex Mercer were present, their faces reflecting a mix of concern and determination.

"I wanted to bring you all up to speed," Jake began. "Lily has uncovered an illegal betting ring connected to high-level figures, including Richard Stanton."

Gasps and murmurs filled the room.

"Stanton?" Sarah repeated. "He's one of the most powerful men in racing."

"Exactly," Jake affirmed. "And they're targeting us. Our unpredictability threatens their operations."

Alex leaned forward. "We need to expose them, but we'll have to be strategic. Stanton has significant influence."

Emma nodded. "Agreed. We can't risk going public without irrefutable evidence."

"I've been thinking," Jake said. "The Monaco race is high-profile. If they're going to make a move, it'll be here. We can use that to our advantage."

Luis raised an eyebrow. "You want to bait them?"

"In a controlled way," Jake clarified. "If we can catch them in the act of tampering with the race, we'll have the proof we need."

Sarah looked skeptical. "That's a big risk, Jake."

"I know," he acknowledged. "But I can't stand by and let them corrupt the sport we love."

Alex placed a reassuring hand on Jake's shoulder. "We're with you. Whatever you need."

Emma met Jake's eyes. "We'll need to coordinate closely with Lily and possibly involve authorities we can trust."

He agreed. "I'll reach out to Detective Laura Mitchell. She's proven reliable before."

As preparations for the race intensified, Jake and his allies set their plan into motion. Lily continued her investigation, working to infiltrate the betting ring's communications. Detective Mitchell agreed to assist discreetly, understanding the delicacy of exposing someone as powerful as Stanton.

The night before the race, Jake received another anonymous message.

Unknown: Last chance to withdraw. Accidents happen when least expected.

He forwarded the message to Lily and Detective Mitchell. The tension was palpable, but Jake remained resolute.

Early the next morning, Lily burst into the team's garage, her face flushed with urgency.

"I intercepted a message," she announced. "They're planning to sabotage your car during the final pit stop."

Emma's eyes widened. "Do we know how?"

"They've bribed one of the pit crew members to tamper with the fuel mixture," Lily revealed.

Jake's jaw tightened. "Do we know who?"

She shook her head. "Not yet. But we have a plan. Detective Mitchell has placed undercover agents among the pit crews. They'll monitor for any suspicious activity."

Alex nodded. "We need to act as if everything is normal. We can't tip them off."

"Agreed," Jake said. "But we need to protect ourselves."

The race began under clear skies, the streets of Monaco lined with spectators. Jake felt a mix of adrenaline and anxiety as he navigated the tight corners and narrow passages of the iconic circuit.

"You're doing great," Emma's voice came through his earpiece. "Pace yourself."

"Copy that," he replied, overtaking a rival driver with a deft maneuver.

As the laps progressed, Jake maintained a strong position. The scheduled pit stop approached, and his heart pounded in anticipation.

"Remember the plan," Emma reminded him. "We'll be watching closely."

He pulled into the pit lane, the team springing into action with practiced precision. Out of the corner of his eye, Jake noticed a crew member he didn't recognize moving toward the fuel intake.

"Who's that?" he asked quietly.

Emma's voice was tense. "That's not one of ours."

Before the stranger could act, two undercover agents moved in, detaining him swiftly.

"Saboteur neutralized," Detective Mitchell's voice confirmed over a secure channel.

Relief washed over Jake. "Thank you."

"Get back out there," Emma urged. "Finish the race."

He rejoined the track, channeling his focus into the final laps. The crowd's cheers blurred into a distant roar as he pushed *The Phoenix* to its limits.

In a thrilling finish, Jake crossed the line in first place, the victory emblematic of more than just a race—it was a stand against corruption.

After the race, the team gathered in a secluded area of the paddock. Detective Mitchell approached with a satisfied smile.

"We've arrested the saboteur," she reported. "He confessed to working under orders from Stanton."

Lily joined them, her eyes alight with triumph. "We also have recorded communications linking Stanton directly to the betting ring and the sabotage attempt."

Jake exhaled deeply. "We did it."

"Not quite yet," Detective Mitchell cautioned. "We need to apprehend Stanton before he realizes his plan failed."

Just then, a commotion erupted nearby. Richard Stanton, flanked by security, was attempting to leave the venue.

"Stop him!" Detective Mitchell commanded, leading her team toward the fleeing official.

Jake and his team watched as Stanton was intercepted, his protests drowned out by the flurry of law enforcement activity.

"Looks like justice is catching up," Alex remarked.

Emma smiled. "It's about time."

In the days that followed, news of Stanton's arrest and the dismantling of the illegal betting ring dominated headlines. The racing community was shaken, but many expressed relief that the corruption was being purged.

At a press conference, Jake stood alongside Lily, Emma, Alex, and Detective Mitchell.

"Today marks a significant victory for integrity in racing," Jake addressed the assembled media. "We have faced challenges that threatened the very essence of our sport. But together, we have shown that honesty and passion prevail over greed and deceit."

Reporters peppered them with questions about the

investigation, the risks they took, and the impact on the sport's future.

Lily spoke confidently. "Our hope is that this serves as a wake-up call. We must remain vigilant to protect the integrity of racing."

As the conference concluded, Jake felt a mixture of satisfaction and contemplation. The battle had been won, but at what cost?

Chapter 16: Crossroads

The Italian countryside stretched out before Jake as he drove along winding roads, the lush vineyards and rustic villas a blur outside his window. After the tumultuous events in Monaco, he had retreated to a secluded estate owned by an old friend, seeking solitude to process everything that had transpired.

Parking the car near a tranquil lake, he stepped out and inhaled the crisp air. The serene environment contrasted sharply with the chaos that had enveloped his life.

He was joined by Emma, who had flown in to check on him.

"Beautiful, isn't it?" she remarked, standing beside him.

"Peaceful," he agreed. "A nice change of pace."

She studied him carefully. "You've been quiet since Monaco."

He sighed. "I've been thinking."

"About?" she prompted gently.

"Everything," he admitted. "The corruption we've exposed, the risks we've taken... the dangers that seem to follow us."

Emma nodded. "It's been a lot."

He turned to face her. "I love racing, Emma. It's been my dream since I was a kid. But now, I wonder if it's worth the toll it's taking."

She placed a hand on his arm. "You're considering walking away."

He looked out over the lake. "Part of me wants to continue, to chase the championship and prove that we can overcome any obstacle. But another part of me is tired—tired of the threats, the manipulation, the constant vigilance."

Emma's eyes softened. "No one would blame you for stepping back. You've done more than most would dare."

"I don't want to abandon the team," he said. "Or the fans who believe in us."

"Then maybe it's about finding balance," she suggested. "Setting boundaries to protect yourself while still pursuing your passion."

He considered her words. "How do I do that when the dangers seem unavoidable?"

"By choosing your battles," she advised. "Not every fight has to be yours alone."

He took a deep breath. "I suppose you're right."

Just then, his phone buzzed with a message from Lily.

Lily: Urgent. Call me as soon as you can.

Concern flashed across his face. "It's Lily. She says it's urgent."

He dialed her number. "Lily, what's wrong?"

"Jake," she began, her voice strained. "There's been a development. Some of Stanton's associates are still at large, and they've issued threats against you."

His grip tightened on the phone. "What kind of threats?"

"Retaliation," she explained. "They blame you for bringing down their operation. I've spoken to Detective Mitchell—she recommends laying low for a while."

Jake's jaw clenched. "I can't keep running."

Emma leaned in, listening.

"Your safety is paramount," Lily insisted. "We can handle things on our end."

He sighed. "Alright. Keep me updated."

After ending the call, he turned to Emma. "It's never-ending."

She touched his shoulder reassuringly. "Maybe it's time to make a choice."

Over the next few days, Jake grappled with his decision. He spent hours reflecting, walking through the vineyards, and considering his future.

One evening, he sat down with Alex Mercer, who had joined them at the estate.

"I hear you're at a crossroads," Alex said, sipping a glass of wine.

"Word travels fast," Jake replied with a faint smile.

Alex chuckled. "Emma filled me in. Thought I might offer some perspective."

"I'm all ears."

"I walked away from racing when the corruption became too

much," Alex began. "But I always wondered if I made the right choice."

"Do you regret it?" Jake asked.

"Sometimes," Alex admitted. "I miss the thrill, the competition. But I found other ways to fulfill my passion—mentoring young drivers, advocating for clean racing."

Jake considered this. "So you think I should step back?"

"I think you need to follow your own path," Alex advised. "But remember, you've already made a significant impact. Your legacy isn't defined solely by championships."

"I just don't want to live in fear," Jake confessed. "Or put those I care about in danger."

Alex nodded. "Then perhaps it's time to redefine your relationship with racing."

The next morning, Jake gathered Emma, Alex, and Lily—who had arrived overnight—in the estate's courtyard.

"I've made a decision," he announced. "I'm going to step away from professional racing for a while."

Emma's eyes filled with understanding. "We support you."

Lily approached him. "Are you sure?"

He nodded. "I need time to reassess, to heal, and to figure out how I can contribute without compromising my safety or well-being."

Alex smiled warmly. "I think that's wise."

"But I don't want to abandon our mission," Jake continued. "I want to use my experience to help others—to mentor young drivers, advocate for integrity in the sport, and support initiatives that promote fair competition."

Emma's face lit up. "You'd be amazing at that."

Lily agreed. "Your voice carries weight. You can inspire real change."

He felt a sense of relief washing over him. "It's not an easy choice, but it's the right one for me now."

They spent the rest of the day discussing plans—how Jake could leverage his platform, the projects they could undertake together, and ways to continue their fight against corruption from a different angle.

Months later, Jake stood before a crowd at a racing academy's opening ceremony. Cameras flashed as he took the podium.

"Welcome to the Turner Racing Academy," he began, a genuine smile spreading across his face. "Our mission is to nurture talent, instill values of integrity, and foster a love for racing that's grounded in respect and sportsmanship."

The audience erupted in applause.

He continued, "Racing has given me so much, and now it's my turn to give back. Together, we'll build a future where the sport thrives free of corruption and fear."

Among the attendees, Emma, Lily, Alex, and his former team members watched proudly.

After the ceremony, Jake mingled with aspiring drivers, their excitement reminding him of his own beginnings.

"Mr. Turner," a young woman approached shyly. "Your story inspires me. I want to race for the right reasons."

He smiled warmly. "Call me Jake. And I'm glad to hear that. We're here to help you achieve your dreams."

As the event wound down, Jake felt a renewed sense of purpose. The path he had chosen was different from what he had once envisioned, but it was fulfilling in ways he hadn't anticipated.

Later that evening, he and his closest allies gathered at a quiet restaurant.

"To new beginnings," Emma toasted, raising her glass.

"To making a difference," Lily added.

"To Jake," Alex concluded. "For choosing his own road."

They clinked glasses, a moment of camaraderie solidifying their shared journey.

Jake looked around the table, gratitude filling his heart. "I couldn't have done any of this without you."

"You've taught us as much as we've supported you," Emma replied.

Lily leaned in. "So, any regrets?"

He thought for a moment before shaking his head. "No. This feels right."

As they shared stories and laughter, Jake realized that while he had stepped away from the racetrack, he hadn't left behind what mattered most—the passion for racing, the drive for integrity, and the connections forged through adversity.

He had reached a crossroads and chosen a path that honored his values and aspirations. The future was uncertain, but he faced it with confidence, surrounded by those who believed in him.

And in that, he found peace.

Chapter 17: The Setup

The evening sky over Suzuka Circuit was a canvas of deep purples and oranges, the sun casting its last golden rays over the storied track. The Japanese Grand Prix was just days away, marking the biggest race of the season and the culmination of months of intense competition. Despite stepping away from professional racing, Jake Turner found himself back in the heart of the action, drawn by a sense of duty he couldn't ignore.

Jake stood at the edge of the pit lane, the familiar scents of fuel and rubber stirring a mix of nostalgia and apprehension. He had returned not as a driver, but as an ally in a covert operation to expose the remnants of the corrupt network that still plagued the sport.

"Never thought I'd see you back here," Emma said, approaching him with a cautious smile.

Jake turned to face her. "Trust me, I didn't plan on it. But sometimes the fight finds you, whether you're ready or not."

She nodded, her eyes reflecting understanding. "Lily filled me in. It's worse than we thought, isn't it?"

"Yes," he confirmed. "Despite our efforts, the network has restructured. They're more insidious now, infiltrating teams and manipulating outcomes discreetly."

Emma crossed her arms, concern etched on her face. "So what's the plan?"

Before Jake could respond, Lily Chen joined them, her expression determined. "Glad you're both here. We have a lot to discuss."

They retreated to a secluded meeting room within the racing complex, where Alex Mercer and Detective Laura Mitchell awaited them.

"Thank you all for coming," Lily began, spreading out a series of documents and blueprints on the table. "We've gathered intelligence that the corrupt network plans to rig the outcome of the Japanese Grand Prix. They're using advanced technology to interfere with cars remotely, ensuring their chosen driver wins."

Alex chimed in. "They've developed a device that can disrupt engine performance. It's virtually undetectable and can be activated from a distance."

Detective Mitchell added, "We've identified several key operatives embedded within various teams, posing as technicians and support staff."

Jake leaned forward. "So they can sabotage any car they choose without raising suspicion."

"Exactly," Lily confirmed. "But we have a window of opportunity. If we can expose them during the race, we can provide undeniable proof of their activities."

Emma glanced around the table. "But how do we do that without endangering the drivers?"

Jake met her gaze. "We set a trap. Use ourselves as bait."

Alex raised an eyebrow. "You're willing to put yourself on the line again?"

He nodded resolutely. "I didn't come back here to watch from the sidelines. If we can draw them out, we can catch them in the act."

Detective Mitchell unfolded a schematic of the pit area. "We've coordinated with race officials who are trustworthy. We'll have undercover agents stationed throughout the facility. Our goal is to intercept the signal from their device and trace it back to the source."

Lily pointed to a specific area on the map. "We believe their control center is located in an unmarked trailer near the service entrance. If we can access it during the race, we can gather the evidence we need."

Emma frowned. "But accessing it won't be easy, especially with heightened security."

Alex smiled slyly. "Leave that part to me. I still have a few tricks up my sleeve."

Jake took a deep breath. "I'll need to get back behind the wheel."

Emma looked at him sharply. "Jake, are you sure? You've been out of the circuit for months."

"I've been training," he assured her. "And besides, they won't expect me to be a participant. It gives us an element of surprise."

Lily considered this. "He's right. His sudden re-entry could disrupt their plans and force them to act, giving us the opportunity to catch them."

Detective Mitchell nodded. "I'll arrange for a wildcard entry. Given Jake's reputation, it won't raise too many eyebrows."

Emma sighed, relenting. "Alright. But we're doing this together. We can't afford any missteps."

Jake gave her a reassuring smile. "Wouldn't have it any other way."

The days leading up to the race were a whirlwind of preparation. Jake reacquainted himself with *The Phoenix*, his car meticulously maintained by Sarah and Luis, who were thrilled to be back in action.

"Feels like old times," Luis remarked, handing Jake a wrench.

Jake chuckled. "Except this time, we're on a mission."

Sarah adjusted her glasses, peering at the engine diagnostics. "All systems are optimal. We've also installed a countermeasure device to detect and block any external interference."

"Good thinking," Jake praised. "We need every advantage we can get."

As word spread of Jake's unexpected return, the media buzzed with speculation. Reporters clamored for interviews, but he kept a low profile, focusing on the task ahead.

In a quiet moment, he found himself standing alone on the track under the stars, the grandstands empty and silent.

"Second thoughts?" Lily's voice broke the stillness.

He turned to see her approaching. "Just reflecting."

She joined him, the two of them gazing out over the illuminated circuit. "You didn't have to come back."

"I know," he replied softly. "But if we can finally put an end to this corruption, it's worth it."

She placed a hand on his arm. "Just promise me you'll be careful."

He smiled gently. "I will."

Race day arrived, the atmosphere electric with anticipation. The stands were packed with fans waving banners and flags, the air alive with the roar of engines and excited chatter.

Jake donned his racing suit, the familiar weight settling comfortably on his shoulders. As he walked toward *The Phoenix*, Emma intercepted him.

"Everything is set," she informed him. "Our agents are in position. Alex is ready to infiltrate the control center."

He nodded. "And the team?"

"Fully briefed and prepared," she assured him. "We've got your back."

He took a deep breath. "Let's make this count."

Climbing into the cockpit, he felt a surge of adrenaline. The engine hummed to life, a powerful reminder of why he loved racing.

"Comm check," Sarah's voice came through his earpiece.

"Loud and clear," he responded.

"Remember, we'll be monitoring for any interference," she reminded him.

"Understood."

As the cars lined up on the grid, Jake's presence drew curious glances from other drivers. Among them was **Damien Wolfe**, a rival known for his aggressive tactics and rumored ties to the corrupt network.

"Didn't expect to see you here, Turner," Damien sneered over the comm channel.

"Thought I'd join the fun," Jake replied coolly.

"Careful you don't get in over your head," Damien warned.

"I could say the same to you."

The lights above the starting line ignited, each one illuminating in succession. The moment they all turned green, the thunderous start of the race erupted.

Jake launched forward, seamlessly blending into the pack. He navigated the twists and turns with precision, his instincts sharp despite his hiatus.

"You're holding steady," Emma updated. "No signs of interference yet."

"Copy that," he acknowledged.

As the race progressed, Jake strategically positioned himself near the front. He noticed Damien maneuvering aggressively, attempting to force him into errors.

"Damien's making his move," he reported.

"Stay focused," Emma advised. "Remember the goal."

Suddenly, a warning light flashed on his dashboard.

"Sarah, I'm getting a systems alert," he informed them.

"Checking now," she responded, her fingers flying over the keyboard. "There's an external signal attempting to access your engine controls."

"Countermeasures activated," Luis announced.

The alert subsided, and Jake breathed a sigh of relief.

"Good work," he praised.

Meanwhile, Alex and Lily moved covertly toward the unmarked trailer. Dressed as maintenance workers, they blended into the background.

"Approaching the target," Alex whispered into his comm.

"Security is light," Lily observed. "They must be confident."

They reached the trailer's entrance, and Alex deftly picked the lock. Inside, they found a sophisticated setup—computers, monitors displaying live race feeds, and devices emitting signals.

"Jackpot," Alex murmured.

Lily began recording with a hidden camera. "We need to download their data."

As they worked, footsteps sounded outside.

"Someone's coming," she warned.

They ducked behind equipment as two men entered, conversing in hushed tones.

"Is the device affecting Turner's car?" one asked.

"It should be," the other replied. "But we're getting interference."

"Boost the signal. We can't let him win."

Alex and Lily exchanged glances. This was the evidence they needed.

Back on the track, Jake felt another surge of interference.

"They're trying again," he reported.

"Countermeasures are holding," Sarah assured him. "But they're increasing power."

"Hang in there, Jake," Emma encouraged.

Damien closed in on him, attempting a dangerous overtake.

"He's getting reckless," Jake noted.

"Let him pass if you need to," Emma advised.

"No," Jake decided. "I have an idea."

He allowed Damien to draw alongside him, then subtly shifted his position, causing Damien to overcompensate. Damien's car veered slightly, and he lost momentum.

"Nice move," Luis cheered.

"Just bought us some time," Jake replied.

In the trailer, Alex and Lily continued collecting data. The men were preoccupied with their sabotage efforts.

"Time to shut them down," Alex whispered.

He signaled to Detective Mitchell, who was standing by with her team.

"Go," Lily confirmed.

Within moments, law enforcement officers stormed the trailer.

"Freeze! Hands where we can see them!"

The men were caught off guard, their expressions shifting from shock to anger.

"What is this?" one demanded.

"You're under arrest for conspiracy to commit fraud and endangerment," Detective Mitchell declared.

Lily stepped forward. "We have everything recorded."

The men glared at her. "You'll pay for this."

"Tell it to the judge," she retorted.

With the control center dismantled, the interference ceased.

"All clear, Jake," Emma reported triumphantly. "They've been taken down."

A smile spread across his face. "Then let's finish this race."

He poured on the speed, *The Phoenix* responding flawlessly. The crowd's excitement escalated as he battled for the lead.

In the final laps, it was down to Jake and Damien. Without the corrupt network's assistance, Damien struggled to maintain his edge.

"Time to show them what real racing looks like," Jake said.

He executed a perfect overtake on the outside of a tight corner, leaving Damien behind.

"Yes!" Emma exclaimed. "You're in the lead!"

The checkered flag waved as Jake crossed the finish line first. The grandstands erupted in cheers, the victory symbolic of a greater triumph.

In the post-race press conference, Jake stood before a sea of reporters.

"Jake, how does it feel to win after your time away?" one asked.

He smiled thoughtfully. "This victory isn't just about me. It's about restoring integrity to the sport we all love. Today, we proved that perseverance and teamwork can overcome even the most entrenched corruption."

Another reporter pressed, "There are rumors of a criminal network being dismantled today. Can you comment?"

Jake exchanged a glance with Lily, who nodded subtly.

"Yes," he confirmed. "Thanks to the efforts of dedicated individuals, we uncovered and stopped a group attempting to manipulate race outcomes. Racing should be about skill, passion, and fair competition. Anything less is unacceptable."

The room buzzed with excitement as the implications sank in.

Later, in a quiet moment away from the spotlight, Jake reunited with his team.

"You did it," Sarah said, beaming.

"We all did," he corrected. "Couldn't have asked for a better team."

Alex approached, clapping him on the back. "Not bad for a retired driver."

Jake laughed. "Maybe I've still got a few laps left in me."

Emma joined them, her eyes reflecting pride and relief. "So what's next?"

He looked around at his friends—his extended family. "I think it's time to find a balance. Maybe I don't have to choose between racing and making a difference. Maybe I can do both."

Lily smiled warmly. "Sounds like the best of both worlds."

He nodded. "With the corrupt network exposed, perhaps we can focus on rebuilding trust in the sport."

Detective Mitchell approached the group. "I wanted to thank you all. Your courage and cooperation were instrumental in bringing these criminals to justice."

"Just doing our part," Jake replied humbly.

She extended her hand. "The sport needs more people like you."

As the team celebrated their success, Jake felt a renewed sense of purpose. The road ahead would undoubtedly hold new challenges, but for the first time in a long while, he felt hopeful.

Standing under the glow of the setting sun, he realized that the true victory wasn't just crossing the finish line—it was standing up for what was right, alongside those who shared his vision.

"To new beginnings," he toasted, raising a bottle of water.

"To integrity and passion," Emma added.

"To the team," Sarah and Luis chimed in.

They clinked their bottles, laughter and camaraderie filling the air.

Jake looked out at the track one last time. "Guess I'm not done with racing after all."

"And racing isn't done with you," Lily replied with a wink.

As night enveloped Suzuka Circuit, the team walked away together, ready to embrace whatever the future held—united, resilient, and committed to making a difference both on and off the track.

Chapter 18: Race Against Time

The morning sun bathed the Valencia Street Circuit in a warm glow, casting long shadows across the asphalt. The final race of the season was upon them, and the atmosphere was electric. Jake Turner stood in the garage beside *The Phoenix*, his eyes reflecting both determination and anticipation.

After their successful operation at Suzuka, Jake had decided to return to professional racing. The sport was regaining its integrity, and he wanted to be part of its renaissance. His performance throughout the season had been exceptional, placing him as a top contender for the championship title. This race would determine everything.

Emma approached, clipboard in hand. "All systems are go," she reported with a smile. "Sarah and Luis have done an amazing job tuning the car."

Jake nodded appreciatively. "I couldn't ask for a better team."

As they prepared for the day's practice sessions, Lily arrived, her expression serious. "Jake, can we talk?"

"Sure," he replied, sensing the urgency in her voice.

They stepped aside from the bustling garage. "I've been digging into the remnants of the corrupt network," she began. "It seems that while we dismantled a significant part, the main antagonist is still out there."

Jake frowned. "Who is it?"

"I'm not certain yet," she admitted. "But I have a lead. I believe someone high up has been orchestrating events from the shadows."

He sighed. "So it's not over."

"No," she confirmed. "But for now, focus on the race. I'll keep you updated."

"Thanks, Lily. Be careful."

As the day progressed, practice went smoothly. *The Phoenix* performed flawlessly, and Jake felt confident.

That evening, the team gathered for a final briefing. "Everything looks good," Emma said. "Get some rest, everyone. Tomorrow's a big day."

Jake stayed behind for a while, going over some last-minute details with Sarah and Luis. "I'm going to do a final check on the car," he told them.

"Need any help?" Luis offered.

"I've got it," Jake assured him.

After they left, Jake walked around *The Phoenix*, inspecting every inch. Satisfied, he locked up the garage and headed back to the hotel.

In the quiet hours before dawn, shadows moved within the garage. Unseen hands tampered with the car, deftly sabotaging critical components before slipping away into the darkness.

The next morning, Jake arrived early at the circuit. The air was crisp, and the scent of the sea lingered. He unlocked the garage and was about to begin his routine checks when something caught his eye.

A small pool of fluid had formed under the car.

"That's odd," he muttered, kneeling to inspect it. His heart sank as he realized it was brake fluid.

"Emma!" he called urgently into his comm.

She arrived moments later, concern etched on her face. "What's wrong?"

"Someone tampered with the car," he said grimly. "Brake lines have been cut, and who knows what else."

She paled. "Sabotage?"

"Looks like it," he confirmed. "We need to fix this before the race."

Emma glanced at the clock. "We have less than four hours."

"Then we'd better get to work," Jake said, determination overriding his frustration.

They summoned Sarah and Luis, who quickly assessed the damage.

"Brake lines are severed," Sarah reported. "Engine wiring has been tampered with, and the fuel mixture has been altered."

"Can we fix it in time?" Jake asked.

Luis exchanged a worried glance with Sarah. "It's going to be tight, but we'll do everything we can."

Emma looked around the garage. "We need to keep this

under wraps. If the saboteur thinks we didn't notice, they won't try anything else."

"Agreed," Jake said. "Let's keep this between us for now."

They sprang into action, each taking on tasks to repair the damage. The clock ticked relentlessly, the pressure mounting with every passing minute.

As Sarah worked on the engine, she shook her head. "Whoever did this knew exactly where to strike. This wasn't random."

Luis nodded. "They wanted to ensure you'd crash or be forced to withdraw."

Jake clenched his jaw. "We need to figure out who did this, but first, we have a race to win."

Meanwhile, Lily continued her investigation. She suspected that the main antagonist was closer than they realized. Accessing security footage from the circuit, she scoured the recordings for any sign of the saboteur.

Her eyes narrowed as she spotted a figure entering the garage in the early hours. Enhancing the image, she recognized **Victor Reynolds**, the disgraced businessman they had previously taken down.

"But that's impossible," she whispered. "He's supposed to be in custody."

She quickly called Detective Mitchell. "Laura, I think Victor Reynolds is behind the sabotage."

"That's not possible," the detective replied. "He's been in

prison awaiting trial."

"Then he must have an accomplice," Lily insisted. "Someone on the inside."

"I'll look into it," Detective Mitchell promised. "In the meantime, be careful."

Back at the garage, the team worked feverishly. Time was running out.

"Brake lines are replaced," Sarah announced.

"Engine wiring restored," Luis added.

"Fuel mixture corrected," Emma confirmed.

Jake checked his watch. "We have thirty minutes before the race starts."

"Let's run a systems check," Sarah suggested.

They powered up *The Phoenix*, monitoring the diagnostics closely.

"Everything's in the green," Sarah said with relief.

Jake exhaled. "Great work, everyone."

As they prepared to head to the starting grid, Lily rushed in.

"Jake, I have news," she said breathlessly.

"Not now," he replied. "We're about to start."

"It's important," she insisted. "I think I know who's behind this."

He paused. "Who?"

"Victor Reynolds. Or someone working for him."

"But Victor's in prison," Jake said, puzzled.

"I know, but I saw someone on the security footage who looks just like him," she explained. "We need to be cautious."

He nodded. "We'll deal with it after the race. Right now, I need to focus."

"Be careful," she urged.

"I will."

The cars lined up on the grid, engines rumbling like thunder. Jake settled into the cockpit, his mind laser-focused.

"Remember, the car is running smoothly, but keep an eye out for anything unusual," Emma's voice came through his earpiece.

"Got it," he replied.

The lights signaled the start, and the race was on.

Jake maneuvered skillfully, gaining positions with each lap. The car responded perfectly, a testament to his team's hard work.

But midway through the race, an alert flashed on his dashboard.

"Engine temperature rising," he reported.

"That's odd," Sarah said. "It was fine during the checks."

"Can you manage it?" Emma asked.

"I'll try," Jake answered, adjusting his driving to reduce strain.

Despite the setback, he maintained a strong position.

Suddenly, the temperature spiked dangerously.

"Something's wrong," he said urgently. "I need to pit."

"Come in," Emma instructed.

He pulled into the pit lane, and the team sprang into action.

"Coolant levels are dropping," Luis observed.

"There's a leak," Sarah exclaimed. "But how?"

Jake clenched his fists. "We must have missed some sabotage."

"We can fix it, but it'll take time," Sarah said.

"Do what you can," he urged.

As they worked, precious seconds ticked away.

"Jake, we have a problem," Emma said quietly. "You're dropping positions."

He took a deep breath. "Just get me back out there."

Minutes later, they patched the leak.

"Go!" Emma shouted.

Jake rejoined the race, now in a lower position.

"There's still time," he told himself.

With renewed determination, he pushed *The Phoenix* to its limits. One by one, he overtook competitors, his skill and focus unwavering.

"You're back in the top five," Emma informed him. "Keep it up."

The final laps approached. Jake was neck and neck with the leader.

"Come on, *The Phoenix*," he whispered. "Just a little more."

In a daring move, he took the inside line on the last corner, surging ahead.

The checkered flag waved as he crossed the finish line first.

"You did it!" Emma cheered.

"Unbelievable!" Sarah exclaimed.

Relief and joy washed over him. "We did it," he said, his voice filled with gratitude.

After the race, amidst the celebrations, Jake gathered his team.

"Thank you all," he said earnestly. "We couldn't have done this without everyone's effort."

Lily approached, her expression serious. "Jake, we need to talk."

He nodded. "Let's step outside."

They moved away from the noise.

"I have more information," she began. "I think I know who the saboteur is."

"Who?" he asked.

"One of our own," she said hesitantly. "Max."

"Max?" Jake repeated, stunned. "But he's been with us from the beginning."

"I know," she said. "But the evidence points to him. He's been in contact with Victor Reynolds' associates."

Jake felt a mixture of disbelief and anger. "Why would he do this?"

"I don't know, but we need to confront him carefully."

He nodded, his mind racing. "We'll handle it. But first, let's keep this between us."

"Agreed," she said.

As they rejoined the festivities, Jake couldn't shake the feeling of betrayal. But he knew they had to act wisely to uncover the truth.

Chapter 19: The Decoy

The following morning, the atmosphere in the team's hospitality suite was subdued. Jake and Lily had shared their suspicions with Emma, who was equally shocked at the possibility of Max's betrayal.

"I can't believe Max would do this," Emma said, her voice barely above a whisper.

"I don't want to believe it either," Jake admitted. "But we need to be sure."

Lily laid out her plan. "We can set a trap. If Max is the mole, we can use false information to flush out the main antagonist."

Emma nodded slowly. "What do you have in mind?"

"I'll plant some false data," Lily explained. "We'll let it slip that Jake has uncovered incriminating evidence against Victor Reynolds and his network, and that he's planning to hand it over to the authorities."

Jake raised an eyebrow. "Won't that put a target on my back?"

"Not if we're careful," she assured him. "We'll monitor Max's communications. If he takes the bait, he'll try to relay the information to his contacts."

Emma considered this. "It's risky, but it could work."

"Do we have any other options?" Jake asked.

They exchanged glances. "No," Emma conceded. "Let's proceed."

Lily crafted a convincing document detailing supposed evidence linking Victor Reynolds to ongoing illegal activities. She encrypted it and placed it on a secure server, then ensured that Max would stumble upon it.

Later that day, Jake approached Max in the garage.

"Hey, Max," he greeted casually. "Can you do me a favor?"

"Sure, Jake," Max replied, his demeanor friendly. "What do you need?"

"I have some files I need to review, but I'm having trouble accessing them remotely," Jake said, handing him a flash drive. "Could you take a look and see if you can get them to open?"

"Of course," Max said, accepting the drive. "I'll check it out."

"Thanks, I appreciate it," Jake said, forcing a smile.

As Max walked away, Jake glanced at Lily, who was observing from a distance. She gave a slight nod, signaling that phase one was complete.

That evening, Lily monitored network activity using specialized software. Sure enough, she detected an outgoing transmission from Max's workstation.

"He's sending the file," she whispered to Jake and Emma, who were gathered around her laptop.

"Can you trace the recipient?" Emma asked.

"Working on it," Lily replied, fingers flying over the keyboard. "Got it. It's being sent to an encrypted address linked to Victor's known associates."

Jake's expression hardened. "So it's true."

Lily continued typing. "I'm intercepting the message and inserting a tracker. This will lead us directly to the main antagonist."

"Good job," Emma said. "Now we wait."

The next morning, Detective Mitchell contacted them. "We received your intel," she said over the secure line. "Our cyber unit traced the tracker to a location on the outskirts of the city. It's a warehouse believed to be a front for criminal activities."

"Are you moving in?" Jake asked.

"We're coordinating a raid," the detective confirmed. "But we need to catch them red-handed."

Lily suggested, "We can set up a meeting. Max can be instructed to deliver the physical evidence in person."

Jake hesitated. "That might put him in danger."

Emma looked at him sharply. "After what he's done, are you really worried about his safety?"

He sighed. "Despite everything, he's still one of us."

Lily nodded. "We can arrange it so that he believes he's making the drop alone, but we'll have backup in place."

"Alright," Jake agreed. "Let's proceed carefully."

As night fell, Max drove to the warehouse, unaware that he was being followed by unmarked police vehicles. He parked and approached the building cautiously.

Inside, Victor Reynolds stood waiting, flanked by two imposing henchmen.

"Do you have it?" Victor asked coldly.

Max swallowed nervously. "Yes," he replied, handing over the flash drive.

Victor examined it, then looked at Max with a sinister smile. "You've done well. But I have one more task for you."

Max shifted uneasily. "What is it?"

"Eliminate Jake Turner," Victor stated bluntly.

Max's eyes widened. "I didn't agree to that."

Victor's expression darkened. "You don't have a choice. You've benefited from our arrangement, and now it's time to repay your debt."

Max stammered, "But... I can't..."

Victor signaled to his henchmen. "Perhaps you need some persuasion."

At that moment, the warehouse doors burst open. "Freeze! Police!" Detective Mitchell shouted, leading a team of officers.

Chaos erupted as Victor's men attempted to flee. Max dropped to the ground, hands over his head.

Victor tried to escape through a side exit, but Jake and Alex were there to intercept him.

"Going somewhere?" Jake asked, blocking his path.

Victor glared at him. "You think you've won?"

"It's over, Victor," Jake said firmly. "You can't keep running."

Police officers converged, and Victor was taken into custody.

Back at the station, Max sat in an interrogation room, head in his hands. Jake entered, the door closing softly behind him.

"Why, Max?" Jake asked quietly.

Max looked up, eyes filled with regret. "They had something on me. They threatened my family."

"You should have come to us," Jake said.

"I was scared," Max admitted. "I thought I could handle it, but it spiraled out of control."

Jake sighed. "You put us all in danger."

"I know," Max said, tears welling up. "I'm so sorry."

"Detective Mitchell is willing to make a deal," Jake informed him. "If you cooperate fully, they might be lenient."

Max nodded. "I'll do whatever it takes to make it right."

In the days that followed, Victor Reynolds was formally charged with multiple offenses, including conspiracy, sabotage, and attempted murder. Max provided valuable testimony that helped dismantle the remaining elements of Victor's network.

The team grappled with mixed emotions. Relief that the threat was finally over, but sadness over Max's betrayal.

During a team meeting, Emma addressed everyone. "We've been through a lot, and it's been tough. But we need to move forward."

Sarah added, "We're stronger now, and we've learned important lessons."

Jake stood before them. "I want to thank all of you for your dedication and resilience. Trust is crucial, and while we've faced challenges, I believe we can rebuild."

Luis raised his hand. "We're with you, Jake. All the way."

There were nods and murmurs of agreement around the room.

Lily stepped forward. "With Victor out of the picture, we can focus on the future."

Emma smiled. "Agreed. Let's get back to what we do best."

A week later, the team gathered at the track for a test session. The atmosphere was lighter, a sense of optimism prevailing.

Jake climbed into *The Phoenix*, feeling a renewed sense of purpose.

"Ready?" Emma's voice crackled in his earpiece.

"Ready," he replied.

As he accelerated down the straightaway, the worries of the past began to fade.

After the session, he joined Lily and Emma on the pit wall.

"Feels good to be back," he said.

Lily nodded. "You've earned it."

Emma looked at them both. "So, what's next?"

Jake grinned. "We focus on racing, on being the best team we can be. No more distractions."

Lily raised an eyebrow. "You sure about that? With us around, there's always an adventure waiting."

He laughed. "True, but maybe we can choose our adventures this time."

They watched as the sun set over the circuit, casting a warm glow.

"To new beginnings," Emma said, extending her hand.

Jake and Lily joined in, their hands stacked together.

"To trust and teamwork," Lily added.

"To the road ahead," Jake finished.

They stood together, united by their experiences and ready to embrace whatever the future held.

Chapter 20: The Unraveling

The city of Barcelona buzzed with life as evening descended, the streets awash with the glow of streetlights and the hum of activity. Jake Turner and Lily Chen sat in a quiet corner of a modest tapas bar, the aroma of sizzling dishes filling the air. They were supposed to be celebrating the recent victories—both on the track and in their ongoing quest to cleanse the sport of corruption. But tonight, an undercurrent of tension dampened their spirits.

Lily leaned in, her voice barely above a whisper. "I've been reviewing the latest data dumps. The corrupt officials we've been tracking are getting nervous. They've started covering their tracks."

Jake sipped his soda, eyes focused. "Do they suspect we're onto them?"

She nodded. "I believe so. Their communication patterns have changed—more encrypted messages, less chatter. They're consolidating resources."

He frowned. "That means they're planning something."

"Exactly," she agreed. "We need to be cautious."

Just then, Jake's phone vibrated on the table. He glanced at the screen—an unknown number. Hesitating for a moment, he answered. "Hello?"

A distorted voice came through. "Mr. Turner, enjoying your evening?"

Jake's grip tightened on the phone. "Who is this?"

"Someone who knows you've been digging where you

shouldn't," the voice replied coldly. "It's time to back off."

Lily watched his expression shift, concern etching her features. "Jake, what's wrong?"

He put the call on speaker. "What do you want?"

"Simple," the voice continued. "Stop your investigation, or there will be consequences."

Jake exchanged a glance with Lily. "We're not intimidated by threats."

A low chuckle emanated from the phone. "Brave words. But bravery won't protect you from what's coming."

The line went dead.

Lily immediately pulled out her laptop. "Let me trace the call."

Jake leaned back, his mind racing. "They've made their move."

She tapped furiously on the keys. "The call was routed through multiple servers, but I might be able to pinpoint the origin."

"Do it," he urged. "We need to know who we're dealing with."

As she worked, Jake scanned the bar. Everything seemed normal, but a nagging feeling told him they were being watched.

"Got it," Lily announced. "The call originated from a building not far from here—a corporate office tied to the racing commission."

Jake's eyes narrowed. "They're closer than we thought."

She looked up, worry creasing her brow. "We should leave. It's not safe here."

He nodded. "Agreed. Let's get back to the hotel and regroup."

They settled the bill and exited the bar, stepping into the cool night air. The streets were still lively, but an undercurrent of tension shadowed their steps.

As they walked, Lily whispered, "We should take a different route, just in case."

"Good idea," Jake replied, adjusting his jacket.

They turned down a side street, the sounds of the main avenue fading behind them. The narrow alley was lined with old buildings, their facades adorned with wrought-iron balconies.

Suddenly, footsteps echoed behind them. Jake glanced over his shoulder, spotting two figures approaching with deliberate pace.

"Lily," he murmured, "we're not alone."

She followed his gaze. "We need to move."

They quickened their pace, but the figures matched their speed. Ahead, another pair of individuals stepped out from a doorway, blocking their path.

Jake's pulse quickened. "Looks like they're not giving us a choice."

The first man spoke, his voice devoid of warmth. "Mr. Turner,

Ms. Chen, we need to have a word."

Jake positioned himself slightly in front of Lily. "If you have something to say, you can do it here."

The second man shook his head. "Our employers insist on a private conversation."

Lily's eyes darted around, assessing their options. "We're not going anywhere with you."

The men exchanged a glance. "I'm afraid this isn't a request."

From the corner of his eye, Jake saw a narrow passage between two buildings. "Lily, on my signal," he whispered.

She gave a subtle nod.

"Now!" he shouted.

They bolted toward the passage, catching their pursuers off guard. The alley was tight and cluttered, but they navigated it swiftly.

"After them!" one of the men yelled.

Jake and Lily emerged onto another street, weaving through the crowd. The festive atmosphere of the city worked to their advantage, providing cover as they dodged between groups of pedestrians.

"We need to split up," Lily suggested. "They can't follow us both."

"Meet at the hotel," Jake agreed. "Stay safe."

She hesitated for a moment, then disappeared into the throng of people.

Jake continued down the street, aware of the footsteps behind him. He turned a corner and ducked into a small courtyard, pressing himself against the wall.

The pursuers rushed past, not noticing his detour.

He exhaled slowly, pulling out his phone to check in with Lily. A message popped up from her: *"Made it back. Where are you?"*

He quickly typed a reply: *"Close. Be there soon."*

Feeling the immediate danger had passed, he made his way back to the hotel, staying vigilant.

When Jake entered the hotel lobby, he spotted Lily waiting by the elevator. Relief washed over her face as she saw him.

"Thank goodness," she said softly. "I was starting to worry."

"Me too," he admitted. "Let's get upstairs."

They rode the elevator in silence, each lost in thought.

Once inside their suite, they secured the door and drew the curtains.

"Whoever these people are, they're serious," Jake stated.

Lily sat at the desk, reopening her laptop. "We need to find out who's behind this and fast."

He agreed. "But we also need to alert Emma and the others. If we're targets, they might be in danger too."

She began typing. "I'll send a secure message to Emma, Alex, and Detective Mitchell."

As she worked, Jake paced the room. "This escalation means we're getting close to something big."

"Or someone," Lily added. "The main orchestrator of the corruption."

Her phone buzzed with a message from Emma: *"Received your alert. We're safe. Heading to a secure location. Keep us updated."*

"At least they're aware," Lily said.

Jake stopped pacing. "We can't keep running. We need to take the fight to them."

She looked up. "Agreed. But how?"

He thought for a moment. "We can set a trap. Use ourselves as bait to draw them out."

She raised an eyebrow. "That's risky."

"Do you have a better idea?" he challenged gently.

She sighed. "No, but we'll need a solid plan."

Jake sat beside her. "We can leverage the race tomorrow. They'll expect me to be there. If we can expose them in front of everyone, they won't be able to hide."

She considered this. "We could use the media to our advantage. Broadcast any evidence we gather in real-time."

"Exactly," he affirmed. "But we'll need help."

She nodded. "I'll reach out to trustworthy contacts in the

press. And we'll coordinate with Detective Mitchell."

"Let's get to work," Jake said, determination hardening his features.

The next morning dawned clear and bright. The Barcelona Circuit was alive with the sounds of engines and the excitement of fans. Jake and Lily arrived early, blending into the bustle of the paddock.

Emma met them at the team's garage, her expression tense. "I don't like this," she admitted. "But I understand why we have to do it."

Alex Mercer joined them, a reassuring presence. "I've arranged for additional security, discreet but effective."

"Thanks, Alex," Jake said. "We'll need all the support we can get."

Lily tapped her earpiece. "I've set up a secure channel with Detective Mitchell. She has officers in plain clothes throughout the venue."

Emma glanced around. "Do we know how they'll make their move?"

"Uncertain," Jake replied. "But if we proceed as usual, they'll reveal themselves."

As the race preparations continued, Jake suited up. The weight of the situation pressed on him, but he pushed it aside, focusing on the task at hand.

"Be careful out there," Emma urged, her eyes reflecting concern.

"I will," he assured her.

Lily gave him a brief smile. "We'll be monitoring everything."

He climbed into *The Phoenix*, the familiar hum of the engine steadying his nerves.

As the race commenced, Jake navigated the track with precision. From the outside, everything appeared normal. But beneath the surface, a silent battle was unfolding.

In the control room, Lily monitored communications. "I'm picking up unusual frequencies," she reported. "Someone's transmitting on a secured channel."

Alex leaned over her shoulder. "Can you intercept?"

"I'm trying," she replied, fingers flying over the keyboard.

On the track, Jake noticed a rival driver, **Marco Silva**, behaving erratically.

"Emma, something's off with Silva," he noted.

"We see it," she confirmed. "Stay alert."

Suddenly, Silva's car swerved dangerously close to Jake's, forcing him to veer sharply to avoid a collision.

"That was too close," Jake muttered.

"Jake, they're trying to take you out," Emma warned.

Back in the control room, Lily exclaimed, "I've cracked the signal. They're coordinating with Silva to force you off the track."

Alex grabbed a headset. "We need to shut this down."

Lily patched into the race officials' communication network. "This is an emergency. Driver Marco Silva is acting under external influence to endanger Jake Turner. We have evidence."

There was a brief pause before the official responded. "Acknowledged. We will intervene."

Moments later, a caution flag was raised, and Silva was ordered to return to the pit lane.

Jake breathed a sigh of relief. "Good work, team."

But the reprieve was short-lived. An explosion rocked the south end of the track, sending plumes of smoke into the air.

"What was that?" Jake exclaimed.

Lily's voice came through urgently. "They've set off a diversion. Reports of a bomb in the hospitality area."

Emma's face paled. "They're escalating."

Alex spoke quickly. "We need to get you off the track, Jake. It's not safe."

He protested. "I can't just abandon the race."

"Your life is more important," Emma insisted.

Reluctantly, Jake complied, bringing *The Phoenix* into the pit lane. Security personnel surrounded him as he exited the car.

As chaos unfolded around them, Lily received a chilling message on her screen: *"You can't escape us. This ends today."*

She showed it to Alex. "They're coming after us directly."

He nodded grimly. "We need to move."

Jake, Lily, Emma, and Alex regrouped in a secure location within the facility. Detective Mitchell joined them, her expression severe.

"We've apprehended Silva," she reported. "He claims he was coerced—his family was threatened."

Jake shook his head. "They're willing to go to any lengths."

Lily's laptop pinged with an alert. "I just detected unauthorized access to our team's server. They're trying to wipe all our data."

Emma groaned. "All our evidence..."

"Not if I can help it," Lily declared, launching into action.

As she worked to counter the cyberattack, Alex stood guard at the door. "We need to be ready in case they try a physical assault."

Detective Mitchell spoke into her radio. "All units, be advised. Protect the Turner team at all costs."

Minutes felt like hours as Lily fought to secure their data. Sweat beaded on her forehead, but her hands remained steady.

"Almost there..." she murmured.

A loud bang echoed from the hallway. Alex tensed. "They're here."

Jake moved to support him. "We won't let them get through."

Emma grabbed a fire extinguisher, her jaw set. "I'm not going down without a fight."

Footsteps approached rapidly. The door shook as someone tried to force it open.

"Hold the door!" Detective Mitchell ordered, drawing her weapon.

The attackers rammed the door again, splintering the frame.

Just as they were about to breach, sirens wailed outside. A voice boomed over a loudspeaker. "This is the police! Drop your weapons and surrender!"

The pounding stopped abruptly. Through the small window, they saw the assailants hesitate, then flee.

Detective Mitchell opened the door cautiously, signaling to the officers who pursued the attackers.

She turned back to the group. "Are you all okay?"

They nodded, relief washing over them.

Lily exhaled deeply. "I secured our data and traced their signal back to a central hub."

Jake looked at her appreciatively. "You're incredible."

She gave a tired smile. "It's not over yet, but we're close."

Over the next few hours, law enforcement raided multiple locations based on Lily's information. High-ranking officials within the racing organization were arrested, their network finally exposed.

At a press conference the following day, Jake stood alongside Lily, Emma, Alex, and Detective Mitchell.

He addressed the gathered media. "We stand here today not just as a racing team but as advocates for integrity and justice. The individuals who sought to undermine the sport we love have been brought to light. This victory belongs to everyone who believes in fair competition."

Lily added, "Technology should enhance our lives, not be a tool for corruption. We will continue to fight against those who misuse it."

The crowd erupted in applause, the sense of triumph palpable.

That evening, the team gathered at a rooftop terrace overlooking the city. The stars twinkled above, a serene contrast to the turmoil they had faced.

Jake raised a glass. "To the best team anyone could ask for. We faced danger head-on and emerged stronger."

Emma clinked her glass against his. "To courage and friendship."

Lily smiled warmly. "And to never backing down from what's right."

Alex grinned. "Here's to hoping our next adventure is a bit less life-threatening."

They laughed, the tension of the past days finally easing.

Jake looked around at his friends, gratitude filling his heart. "I couldn't have done this without you all."

"We're a team," Emma affirmed. "Always."

As they enjoyed the peaceful night, Jake felt a deep sense of fulfillment. The road had been arduous, but they had made a difference.

"What's next?" Lily asked, leaning on the railing.

Jake gazed thoughtfully at the horizon. "We get back to racing, focus on the sport we love. And we stay vigilant."

She nodded. "Agreed. The work continues, but for now, let's enjoy this moment."

They stood together, united by shared trials and triumphs, ready to face whatever the future held with unwavering resolve.

Chapter 21: The Pursuit

The sun had barely set over the city skyline when Jake Turner and Lily Chen found themselves weaving through the crowded streets of Madrid. The vibrant energy of the city was palpable, but tonight, it served as the backdrop for a perilous game of cat and mouse.

Earlier that day, they had received an anonymous tip about a clandestine meeting of the remaining members of the corrupt network they had been battling. Determined to gather evidence and finally bring down the shadowy figures pulling the strings, Jake and Lily decided to surveil the meeting location—a secluded warehouse on the outskirts of the city.

Armed with discreet recording devices and a plan to remain unseen, they had positioned themselves in an adjacent building, observing through binoculars as influential figures arrived under the cover of darkness.

"That's definitely **Marco Alvarez**," Lily whispered, capturing images of the notorious fixer known for his deep connections in the underworld.

"And there's **Elena Rossi**, head of the European Racing Commission," Jake noted grimly. "I can't believe she's involved at this level."

Their quiet triumph was short-lived. A sudden flash of movement caught Jake's eye. "Lily, did you see that?"

Before she could respond, the door behind them burst open. A burly man filled the doorway, his silhouette ominous against the dim light. "Found you," he growled.

"Run!" Jake shouted, grabbing Lily's hand. They bolted down

the narrow corridor, the sound of heavy footsteps pursuing them.

They burst onto the fire escape, descending the metal stairs as quickly as they dared. Reaching the alley below, they sprinted toward the bustling main street, hoping to lose their pursuers in the crowd.

"Split up!" Lily urged. "We'll meet at the Plaza Mayor."

"Be careful," Jake warned, veering left as Lily headed right.

The labyrinthine streets of Madrid became a maze as Jake navigated through alleyways and side streets. He could hear the shouts of the men chasing him, their determination evident.

Dodging pedestrians and leaping over obstacles, Jake's mind raced. He needed to reach a safe location and contact Emma and Alex for assistance. He darted into a subway station, weaving through the throng of commuters.

Behind him, the pursuers were relentless. Jake boarded a train just as the doors closed, offering a momentary reprieve. Catching his breath, he pulled out his phone to text Lily.

Jake: On the train heading north. Are you safe?

Moments later, a reply came.

Lily: I'm okay. Heading to the rendezvous point. Watch your back.

As the train slowed at the next station, Jake noticed two men scanning the carriages. They spotted him, eyes narrowing.

"How did they—?" Jake muttered, realizing they must have coordinated with others. He pushed through the crowd, exiting the train and racing up the stairs to the street above.

The chase intensified as he dashed into a market filled with stalls and shoppers. The vibrant colors and lively chatter contrasted sharply with the urgency of his situation.

Spotting a delivery truck unloading goods, Jake seized the opportunity. He slipped behind it, then quickly climbed into the back, hiding among the crates.

Holding his breath, he listened as the footsteps of his pursuers grew louder, then faded as they moved past.

After a few tense minutes, the truck driver returned, oblivious to his new passenger. The vehicle rumbled to life, merging into the flow of traffic.

Jake peeked out cautiously, estimating that he was a few blocks from the Plaza Mayor. Deciding it was safe to disembark, he waited until the truck slowed at a corner, then jumped down, blending into the sidewalk traffic.

Meanwhile, Lily navigated her own obstacles. After splitting from Jake, she had used her knowledge of the city to her advantage, slipping through narrow alleys and utilizing back entrances of shops.

She contacted Alex, briefing him on the situation. "We were compromised. They must have known we were coming."

"Meet me at the safe house," Alex instructed. "I've alerted Emma and Detective Mitchell."

"Understood," Lily replied, adjusting her course.

As she approached the plaza, she noticed an unusual number

of street performers and vendors. Something felt off.

Her instincts proved correct when a group of men began closing in from different directions. Recognizing the threat, Lily ducked into a nearby museum, weaving through the exhibits as she sought an exit.

Exiting through a side door, she found herself in a quiet courtyard. Her relief was short-lived as two figures emerged, blocking her path.

"Ms. Chen, you're proving to be quite elusive," one of them sneered.

Lily assessed her surroundings. "What do you want?"

"Your interference ends now," the other man declared, advancing toward her.

Before they could act, a motorcycle roared into the courtyard. The rider, clad in a helmet, skidded to a stop between Lily and her assailants.

"Get on!" the rider shouted, extending a hand.

Recognizing the voice, Lily didn't hesitate. She jumped onto the back of the motorcycle, wrapping her arms around the rider's waist.

They sped away, leaving the stunned pursuers behind.

"Alex, you have impeccable timing," Lily exclaimed over the wind.

He glanced back briefly. "Couldn't let you have all the fun."

Jake arrived at the safe house—a modest apartment tucked away in a residential neighborhood. Emma opened the door, her expression a mix of worry and relief.

"Thank goodness you're safe," she said, ushering him inside.

"Any word from Lily?" he asked anxiously.

"She's with Alex. They're on their way," Emma assured him.

As they waited, Jake filled her in on the events. "They were prepared for us. It's like they knew our every move."

Emma frowned. "We must have a leak somewhere."

"Agreed," Jake said. "But right now, we need to regroup."

A short while later, Alex and Lily arrived. Reunited, the team convened around the dining table.

"They're getting bolder," Alex observed. "Attacking in public without fear of exposure."

Lily nodded. "They must be desperate. We're closing in on them."

"Did you manage to secure any evidence?" Emma inquired.

Lily's face fell. "No, they interrupted before we could collect anything substantial."

Jake leaned forward. "We need a new strategy. They're onto us, and they're not holding back."

"Perhaps it's time to lure them out on our terms," Alex suggested.

Emma raised an eyebrow. "How do you propose we do that?"

"We can use ourselves as bait," Lily proposed. "Set up a fake meeting with a 'source' claiming to have damaging information against them."

Jake considered this. "It's risky, but it might be our best shot."

Alex agreed. "We'll need to control the environment—ensure we have backup and escape routes."

"Detective Mitchell can assist," Emma added. "She has resources here in Spain."

"Then it's settled," Jake said decisively. "Let's plan the setup."

Chapter 22: Collision

The following day, the team meticulously arranged the fake meeting. They chose an abandoned hotel slated for demolition, providing ample opportunities for surveillance and control.

Lily sent out encrypted messages to known contacts within the corrupt network, hinting at a whistleblower ready to expose critical information.

As evening approached, the team took their positions. Alex coordinated with local law enforcement, ensuring they were poised to intervene.

Jake stood in the dimly lit lobby of the hotel, posing as the whistleblower's representative. Dressed inconspicuously, he awaited the arrival of the antagonists.

Through his earpiece, Lily's voice came through. "We have movement. Three vehicles approaching from the east."

"Understood," Jake replied calmly.

Emma, stationed on the hotel's second floor, monitored the security feeds. "They're entering the building. Stay sharp."

The doors swung open as **Marco Alvarez** and his entourage entered. Marco's sharp features were set in a predatory smile. "Mr. Turner, I was surprised to hear from you."

Jake met his gaze evenly. "I represent someone who wants to make a deal."

"Is that so?" Marco drawled, circling slowly. "And where is this mysterious individual?"

"They'll reveal themselves once terms are agreed upon," Jake stated.

Marco chuckled. "You must think I'm foolish. Walking into a trap, perhaps?"

Jake remained composed. "You're free to leave if you don't trust me."

"Ah, but where's the fun in that?" Marco signaled to his men. "Search the building."

As his henchmen dispersed, Lily whispered urgently, "They're sweeping the area. They might find us."

Alex responded, "Stay hidden. We need to let this play out a bit longer."

Back in the lobby, Marco's demeanor shifted. "You know, Jake, you've been quite a thorn in our side."

"Just doing what's right," Jake retorted.

Marco's eyes hardened. "Right and wrong are subjective. Power, however, is absolute."

From the shadows, a new voice emerged. "Perhaps, but your time wielding it is over."

Jake turned to see **Victor Reynolds** step forward, a smug expression on his face.

"Victor?" Jake exclaimed. "But you're supposed to be in custody!"

Victor laughed. "Did you really think it would be that easy to keep me locked away? Money can buy many things—including freedom."

Emma's voice came through urgently. "Jake, we didn't anticipate Victor's involvement. Be careful."

Jake squared his shoulders. "So, the mastermind reveals himself."

Victor smirked. "I prefer 'visionary.' You and your meddling friends have been quite the nuisance."

"Your reign ends tonight," Jake declared.

Victor raised an eyebrow. "Bold words for a man surrounded."

At his signal, more armed men emerged, encircling Jake.

"Time to eliminate the problem once and for all," Victor said coldly.

Before they could act, the sound of sirens pierced the air.

Alex's voice boomed over a loudspeaker. "This is the police! Drop your weapons and surrender!"

Chaos erupted as law enforcement officers stormed the building. A firefight ensued between the criminals and the police.

Jake took cover behind a pillar, searching for an escape route.

"Jake, get to the stairwell!" Lily directed. "We'll cover you."

He sprinted toward the stairs, dodging debris and crossfire. Reaching the second floor, he reunited with Lily and Emma.

"Victor's here," he informed them breathlessly.

"We know," Emma replied. "We need to get out before this place becomes a war zone."

They moved swiftly through the corridors, Alex coordinating their exit.

"There's an unmarked van waiting behind the building," he instructed. "Go now!"

As they navigated the maze-like interior, a sudden explosion rocked the structure.

"They're trying to bring the building down!" Lily exclaimed.

Jake grabbed her hand. "We have to keep moving!"

They reached the rear exit, bursting into the alley where the van awaited. Piling inside, they sped away as the hotel began to collapse behind them.

"Everyone okay?" Alex asked from the driver's seat.

"All accounted for," Emma confirmed, though her eyes reflected the gravity of their escape.

Jake glanced back at the cloud of dust enveloping the area. "They were willing to destroy an entire building to get to us."

Lily's expression was somber. "They're more desperate than ever."

Alex's phone rang. He answered quickly. "Detective Mitchell, what's the situation?"

Her voice was strained. "We managed to apprehend several of Victor's men, but he escaped in the chaos. We're issuing an international warrant, but he's gone underground."

Jake clenched his fists. "He won't stop until he's taken down everything I care about."

As if on cue, his personal phone buzzed with a message from an unknown number.

Unknown: You can't protect them all, Jake. Your family is next.

A chill ran down his spine. "No..."

Emma noticed his distress. "What is it?"

He showed them the message. "He's threatening my family."

Lily placed a reassuring hand on his shoulder. "We'll do everything we can to keep them safe."

"Alex, get us to the airport," Jake ordered. "I need to get back home."

Hours later, they arrived in Jake's hometown—a quiet suburb where his parents and younger sister lived. The familiar streets now seemed fraught with danger.

They pulled up to his family's house, and Jake hurried to the door, knocking urgently.

His mother, **Margaret Turner**, opened the door, surprise turning to concern at the sight of him. "Jake? What's wrong?"

"Mom, I need you, Dad, and Jenna to pack some things quickly. We have to leave."

She looked past him to the others. "Jake, what's going on?"

"There's no time to explain. Please, trust me."

His father, **Robert Turner**, appeared behind Margaret. "Son, you're scaring us."

Jake took a deep breath. "Dad, you're all in danger. We need to get you to a safe place."

Robert exchanged a worried glance with Margaret. "Alright, we'll do as you say."

As his parents moved to gather essentials, Jake pulled Emma aside. "We need to secure the perimeter. I don't know how much time we have."

She nodded, signaling to Alex and Lily. "We'll set up surveillance."

Jenna, Jake's teenage sister, emerged from her room, confusion etched on her face. "Jake? Why are you here?"

He hugged her tightly. "Just a precaution, sis. We're going on a little trip."

She pulled back, studying his face. "You're not telling me something."

He forced a reassuring smile. "I'll explain everything soon."

Suddenly, a loud crash sounded from the front of the house. The living room window shattered as a smoke canister rolled across the floor.

"Get down!" Jake shouted, pulling Jenna to the ground.

Men in tactical gear swarmed through the broken window and door.

"Move! Move!" Jake commanded, guiding his family toward the back exit.

Alex and Emma engaged the intruders, using non-lethal force to incapacitate them.

"Head to the garage!" Alex yelled.

They scrambled into the garage, piling into the family's SUV. Jake started the engine as bullets ricocheted off the metal door.

"Hold on!" he warned, crashing through the garage door into the street.

Lily navigated from the passenger seat. "Take the next left!"

Margaret clutched Jenna, fear evident. "Jake, what's happening?"

He glanced at them in the rearview mirror. "I'm sorry, Mom. I've brought trouble to our doorstep."

Robert spoke firmly. "We'll face it together."

As they sped away, two black SUVs appeared in pursuit.

"They're gaining on us," Emma observed, checking the side mirror.

"Any ideas?" Jake asked, swerving to avoid oncoming traffic.

Alex radioed ahead. "I have contacts setting up a roadblock. We need to lead them there."

Lily coordinated with their allies. "Take the highway ramp ahead."

Jake accelerated onto the highway, the pursuing vehicles closing in.

"Everyone, brace yourselves," he instructed.

Up ahead, police vehicles blocked the road. Jake veered sharply onto an exit ramp, the SUVs following blindly.

As they rounded a curve, the lead SUV lost control, flipping dramatically before coming to a halt.

The second vehicle skidded to a stop as law enforcement officers surrounded it.

Jake pulled over safely, exhaling deeply.

His family sat in stunned silence.

Robert broke the tension. "Jake, I think it's time you tell us what's going on."

He nodded, weariness creeping into his voice. "I will, Dad. I promise."

Later, at a secure location provided by Detective Mitchell, Jake sat with his family, recounting the events that had led them there.

Margaret listened intently. "We had no idea you were involved in something so dangerous."

"I'm sorry I didn't tell you sooner," Jake said remorsefully. "I wanted to protect you."

Robert placed a hand on his shoulder. "We're proud of you, son. Standing up against injustice isn't easy."

Jenna hugged him. "Just don't leave us out again."

He smiled softly. "Deal."

Emma approached. "We've received word that Victor's network has been further dismantled. International agencies are now involved."

Lily added, "Victor himself is still at large, but his resources are dwindling."

Jake stood, resolve firming. "I won't let him threaten my family or anyone else again. It's time to finish this."

Alex nodded. "We're with you all the way."

Margaret exchanged a glance with Robert. "And so are we."

He looked at them, surprised. "Mom, Dad, this isn't your fight."

Robert shook his head. "Family stands together."

Touched, Jake embraced them. "Thank you."

As they prepared for the final confrontation, Jake knew that the collision of his personal and professional worlds had made him more determined than ever. With his family and friends by his side, he felt ready to face whatever lay ahead.

Together, they would put an end to the threat once and for all.

Chapter 23: The Final Race

The sun rose over the Monte Carlo harbor, casting a golden hue on the sleek yachts and azure waters. The Monaco Grand Prix—the crown jewel of the racing world—was set to begin, and the atmosphere buzzed with anticipation. Spectators from around the globe filled the grandstands, eager to witness the climax of the season.

In the paddock, Jake Turner stood beside *The Phoenix*, his racing car meticulously prepared for the most important race of his life. Despite the threats and turmoil of recent weeks, he was resolute. This race was not just about winning a championship; it was about confronting his fears, protecting those he loved, and restoring integrity to the sport he cherished.

Emma approached him, her eyes reflecting both concern and admiration. "Are you sure about this?" she asked quietly.

He met her gaze steadily. "I have to do this, Emma. If I back down now, they win."

She nodded, squeezing his arm. "Then we're with you all the way."

Lily joined them, her expression determined. "We've secured the perimeter. Alex and Detective Mitchell have plainclothes officers throughout the venue. If Victor tries anything, we'll know."

"Good," Jake replied. "But our priority is keeping everyone safe."

His parents and sister stood nearby, offering supportive smiles. Margaret Turner stepped forward, placing a gentle hand on his cheek. "Be careful out there, Jake."

He smiled warmly. "I will, Mom."

Robert Turner clapped his son on the shoulder. "Give 'em hell, son."

Jenna grinned. "You're going to be amazing."

As race time approached, Jake donned his helmet, the world narrowing to the familiar confines of the cockpit. The roar of engines filled the air as the cars lined up on the grid.

Through his earpiece, Emma's voice came through clear and steady. "All systems are go. Remember, stay focused. We're monitoring everything."

"Thanks, team," Jake replied, glancing at the row of lights above the starting line.

The red lights illuminated one by one, the tension building. Then, in an instant, they went out, and the race was on.

The Phoenix surged forward, its engine responding flawlessly to Jake's commands. He navigated the tight corners and narrow streets of Monaco with precision, the city's iconic landmarks a blur as he pushed the car to its limits.

"You're in third place," Emma updated. "Pace yourself."

"Copy that," Jake acknowledged, his eyes scanning the road ahead.

As the laps progressed, the competition intensified. **Marco Silva**, reinstated after his coerced involvement was revealed, led the pack, followed closely by **Damien Wolfe**, a fierce rival with everything to prove.

"Damien's right ahead," Emma informed him. "Watch for his

aggressive moves."

"Understood," Jake replied.

Entering the famous Tunnel section, Jake sensed an opportunity. He accelerated, pulling alongside Damien as they emerged into the blinding sunlight.

"Careful, Jake," Lily cautioned. "Damien's been known to block overtakes here."

But Jake was ready. Anticipating Damien's maneuver, he deftly shifted lanes, overtaking him with inches to spare.

"Yes!" Sarah cheered from the pit wall. "You're in second!"

"Great move," Emma praised. "Now focus on closing the gap with Silva."

As he pursued the leader, Jake couldn't shake the feeling that something was amiss. The car's handling felt slightly off—a subtle vibration that hadn't been there before.

"Emma, I'm detecting a slight wobble," he reported. "Can you check the telemetry?"

"Analyzing now," she replied. A moment later, her tone turned serious. "Jake, your rear left tire is losing pressure."

"That's not possible," Sarah interjected. "We checked everything."

"Could it be sabotage?" Jake asked, his mind racing.

Lily's voice cut in. "I'm scanning the data. It looks like a small puncture, but not from debris."

"Stay calm," Emma advised. "We need to make a pit stop."

"I'll lose position," Jake protested.

"If you don't, the tire could blow," Sarah warned. "It's too dangerous."

Weighing his options in a split second, Jake made his decision. "Pitting now."

He guided *The Phoenix* into the pit lane, where his crew awaited. They sprang into action, replacing the tire with practiced efficiency.

"Go, go, go!" Emma shouted.

Rejoining the race, Jake had fallen to fifth place.

"Don't worry," Emma encouraged. "You have time to catch up."

Determination fueled him as he pushed the car harder, shaving seconds off his lap times. One by one, he overtook his competitors, the crowd's excitement palpable.

"You're back in third," Emma updated. "Silva and Damien are ahead."

"Any sign of Victor?" Jake inquired.

"Security reports no sightings," Lily responded. "But stay alert."

With only ten laps remaining, Jake knew he had to make his move. He closed in on Damien, the two cars battling fiercely through the chicanes.

"He's not giving an inch," Jake noted.

"Keep the pressure on," Emma advised. "He might make a

mistake."

As they approached the tight hairpin turn, Damien braked late, trying to maintain his lead. Seizing the moment, Jake slipped inside, overtaking him cleanly.

"Brilliant!" Sarah exclaimed. "Second place!"

"Now for Silva," Jake said, his eyes fixed on the car ahead.

The gap between them narrowed with each lap. With five laps to go, Jake was right on Silva's tail.

"He's defending hard," Emma observed. "Be strategic."

On the penultimate lap, Jake saw his chance. Exiting the Tunnel, he harnessed *The Phoenix*'s power, pulling alongside Silva.

The two cars raced neck and neck along the waterfront. In a daring move, Jake edged ahead, taking the lead as they entered the final lap.

"You're in first!" Emma cheered. "Keep it steady."

But the victory was not yet secured. Suddenly, an alarm sounded in the cockpit.

"Engine temperature rising rapidly," Jake reported.

"That's impossible," Sarah said, confusion evident. "We checked the cooling system thoroughly."

Lily's voice was urgent. "Jake, I think someone's hacking into your car's systems remotely."

"Can you block it?" he asked, tension mounting.

"I'm trying," she replied, fingers flying over her keyboard.

The engine began to sputter, and the car lost speed.

"Come on, *The Phoenix*," Jake urged. "Don't fail me now."

Behind him, Silva and Damien closed in.

"Jake, I've isolated the signal," Lily announced. "It's coming from within the venue."

"Victor," Jake muttered.

"I'm sending a counter-signal," Lily continued. "But I need more time."

"Do what you can," he replied, gripping the wheel tightly.

As he navigated the treacherous turns, Jake relied on his skill and intuition to maintain control. The engine's performance stabilized slightly, but the car was still lagging.

"Silva's about to overtake," Emma warned.

In a bold maneuver, Jake blocked Silva's advance, positioning his car defensively.

"Almost there," Lily said. "Just a few more seconds."

The finish line was in sight, but Damien had gained significant ground.

"Jake, watch out!" Emma shouted.

Damien attempted a reckless overtake on the inside, his car brushing against Jake's. The impact sent *The Phoenix* skidding toward the barrier.

Time seemed to slow as Jake fought to regain control. With extraordinary reflexes, he corrected the skid, steering the car back onto the racing line.

"Yes!" Sarah shouted. "You saved it!"

"Engine back online," Lily confirmed. "I've blocked the hack."

"Go for it, Jake!" Emma encouraged. "This is your moment!"

Summoning every ounce of focus, Jake accelerated toward the finish line. Silva and Damien were mere meters behind, but he held his lead.

The checkered flag waved as Jake crossed the line first, the crowd erupting in thunderous applause.

"You did it!" Emma's voice was filled with joy.

"Congratulations, Jake!" Lily added, relief evident.

He exhaled deeply, a mix of exhaustion and elation washing over him. "We did it, team."

As he completed the cool-down lap, Jake reflected on the journey that had led him here—the challenges faced, the dangers overcome, and the unwavering support of his friends and family.

Back in the paddock, the atmosphere was celebratory. The team gathered around Jake as he emerged from the car.

Margaret embraced him tightly. "We're so proud of you!"

Robert shook his hand firmly. "A well-deserved victory, son."

Jenna jumped with excitement. "You're the champion!"

Emma wiped away a tear. "You were incredible out there."

Sarah and Luis high-fived each other. "Best race ever!"

Lily approached, her eyes reflecting both happiness and concern. "You handled that beautifully."

"Couldn't have done it without you blocking the hack," Jake acknowledged.

Detective Laura Mitchell joined them, her expression serious. "Jake, we have news. Victor Reynolds has been apprehended."

Jake's eyes widened. "When?"

"During the race," she explained. "He was traced to a control room within the venue, attempting to sabotage your car. Thanks to Lily's countermeasures, we caught him in the act."

Relief and satisfaction filled Jake. "That's the best news I've heard all day."

The team cheered, the weight of the past weeks lifting from their shoulders.

Later, at the championship ceremony, Jake stood atop the podium, the trophy gleaming in his hands. The national anthem played as he looked out over the sea of faces—fans who had supported him through thick and thin.

In his acceptance speech, he spoke from the heart. "This victory is not just mine but belongs to everyone who believes in fairness, integrity, and the true spirit of competition. Thank you to my incredible team, my family, and all of you who never stopped believing."

The crowd erupted in applause, the moment a culmination of perseverance and unity.

That evening, the team celebrated at a private gathering overlooking the harbor. Laughter and stories filled the air as they recounted the highs and lows of their journey.

Alex raised a glass. "To Jake, our champion and friend. Your courage inspires us all."

"To the team," Jake replied, lifting his own glass. "We faced every challenge together."

As the night progressed, Jake found a quiet moment on the terrace. Lily joined him, the city lights reflecting in her eyes.

"Quite a day," she remarked.

He smiled. "One I'll never forget."

She hesitated before speaking. "Jake, there's something I need to tell you."

He turned to face her. "What's on your mind?"

She took a deep breath. "I've been offered a position with an international agency focusing on cybersecurity and combating corruption."

"That's amazing," he responded genuinely. "You deserve it."

"But it means I'll be traveling extensively," she continued. "I wanted you to hear it from me first."

He nodded thoughtfully. "I'll miss having you around, but I understand. This is important work."

She smiled softly. "We've come a long way, haven't we?"

"We have," he agreed. "And no matter where we are, we'll always be a team."

They shared a moment of comfortable silence, the bond between them stronger than words.

As the festivities wound down, Jake reflected on the path ahead. The challenges weren't over—there would always be new obstacles, new adversaries. But for now, he felt a profound sense of peace.

Rejoining his family and friends, he embraced the present, grateful for the journey and hopeful for the future.

The final race had tested him in every way possible, but it had also reaffirmed what mattered most: integrity, perseverance, and the unbreakable ties of those who stood by his side.

As the first light of dawn touched the horizon, Jake knew that whatever lay ahead, he was ready to face it—with courage in his heart and a champion's spirit guiding his way.

Chapter 24: Exposed

The morning after his triumphant victory at the Monaco Grand Prix, Jake Turner awoke to the sound of his phone buzzing incessantly. Groggy from the previous night's celebrations, he reached for the device on the bedside table. Dozens of messages and missed calls flashed across the screen.

"Jake, turn on the news!" one text read.

"Did you see what's happening?" another implored.

Confused, Jake sat up and switched on the television. Every channel was broadcasting the same footage—a series of live videos from the race that had gone viral overnight. The headlines were explosive:

"Racing Scandal Unveiled: Conspiracy Exposed During Monaco Grand Prix"

As the footage played, Jake's eyes widened. The live broadcast from the race had inadvertently captured incriminating actions by several high-ranking officials and team members involved in the corrupt network he and his team had been battling.

One clip showed a team manager in a heated exchange with a known associate of Victor Reynolds, passing what appeared to be a data drive. Another angle caught a pit crew member tampering with a competitor's car during a pit stop. The most damning footage showed a race official communicating covertly with a driver, signaling him to engage in dangerous tactics against Jake.

The commentators were in a frenzy. "It appears that the conspiracy runs deeper than anyone suspected," one said.

"These live images suggest a coordinated effort to manipulate race outcomes and endanger drivers."

Jake's phone rang. It was Emma. "Jake, are you seeing this?"

"Yeah," he replied, still processing the information. "I can't believe it."

"Lily is on her way over," Emma informed him. "We need to meet and figure out our next steps."

"Agreed," Jake said. "I'll be at the team's suite in fifteen minutes."

As he dressed hurriedly, Jake's mind raced. How had this footage come to light? And who was responsible for broadcasting it?

At the team's suite, Jake found Emma, Lily, Sarah, and Luis gathered around a large screen displaying the news coverage. Their expressions ranged from shock to grim satisfaction.

"Any idea how this happened?" Jake asked as he entered.

Lily turned to him, her eyes bright with a mix of excitement and concern. "I've been digging into it. It seems that during the race, an anonymous hacker tapped into the live broadcast feeds and overlaid additional camera angles that weren't part of the official coverage."

Emma frowned. "Is that even possible?"

Lily nodded. "With the right skills and access, yes. The hacker managed to stream these additional feeds directly to the broadcast networks, making it appear as part of the live coverage."

Sarah looked puzzled. "But why would someone do that? And who?"

Jake considered this. "Maybe someone on the inside who wanted to expose the corruption but couldn't do it openly."

Lily's fingers flew over her laptop keyboard. "I'm trying to trace the source, but whoever did this covered their tracks well."

Just then, Alex Mercer walked in, his expression serious. "I just spoke with Detective Mitchell. The authorities are scrambling to respond. Arrest warrants are being issued for several individuals caught on camera."

"That's good news," Emma said. "But it also means things could get dangerous. Desperate people do desperate things."

Jake nodded. "We need to be cautious."

Lily looked up from her screen. "I managed to find a clue. The hacker left a digital signature—just a simple symbol: a phoenix rising."

Jake exchanged a glance with the others. "A phoenix?"

"Yes," Lily confirmed. "It's the same symbol we use for *The Phoenix*," she added, referring to Jake's car.

Sarah's eyes widened. "Do you think...?"

At that moment, Jake's phone buzzed with a new message from an unknown number.

Unknown: Sometimes justice needs a little push. Keep fighting the good fight.

He showed the message to the team. "Looks like our anonymous ally is reaching out."

Emma smiled slightly. "Whoever they are, they just gave us a powerful tool against the corruption."

Alex agreed. "With this footage broadcasted to millions, public pressure will force the authorities to act decisively."

Lily tapped her chin thoughtfully. "We should capitalize on this momentum. Let's prepare a statement supporting the investigation and reaffirming our commitment to integrity in racing."

Jake nodded. "Good idea. We need to show leadership during this crisis."

Within hours, Jake and his team held a press conference. Reporters filled the room, eager for comments on the unfolding scandal.

Jake stepped up to the podium, cameras flashing. "Like many of you, I was shocked by the footage that emerged from yesterday's race. It is deeply troubling to see such blatant disregard for the integrity of our sport and the safety of its participants.

"Racing is built on the principles of fair competition, skill, and sportsmanship. Any attempt to undermine these values must be met with swift and decisive action.

"I fully support the ongoing investigations and urge the authorities to leave no stone unturned in bringing those responsible to justice. My team and I remain committed to promoting transparency and integrity in all aspects of racing."

A reporter raised a hand. "Mr. Turner, do you have any idea who might be behind the release of this footage?"

Jake paused thoughtfully. "At this time, we do not know the identity of the individual or individuals who released the footage. However, their actions have shone a light on issues that must be addressed for the good of the sport."

Another reporter asked, "Do you feel that your safety is at risk given these revelations?"

Jake glanced at his team before responding. "Safety is always a concern in this sport, both on and off the track. We are taking appropriate precautions, but our focus remains on working collaboratively to ensure the integrity of racing is upheld."

After the press conference, the team regrouped in a private meeting room. Detective Mitchell joined them via video call.

"We've made several arrests based on the footage," she reported. "The evidence is substantial, and with public outcry, the judiciary is moving quickly."

"That's encouraging," Emma said. "But we still don't know who our mysterious hacker is."

Detective Mitchell smiled slightly. "Actually, I might have some information on that. An informant within the racing commission reached out to me. They claimed responsibility for the leak."

Lily leaned forward. "Who is it?"

"A junior IT specialist named **Elena Martinez**," the detective revealed. "She said she couldn't stand by and watch the corruption continue, so she took matters into her own hands."

Jake was impressed. "That was incredibly brave of her."

"Indeed," Detective Mitchell agreed. "But she's now in protective custody. There are concerns about retaliation from those still at large."

Alex spoke up. "Is there anything we can do to support her?"

"I think a public show of support would be beneficial," the detective suggested. "But we need to be careful not to expose her further."

Jake nodded. "We'll find a way to acknowledge her actions without compromising her safety."

In the days that followed, the racing world was turned upside down. Sponsors withdrew from tainted teams, officials resigned or were suspended pending investigations, and a comprehensive audit of racing operations was launched.

Jake and his team became vocal advocates for reform, participating in meetings with racing authorities and other drivers to establish new protocols aimed at preventing future corruption.

During a televised panel discussion, Jake emphasized the importance of collective responsibility. "We all have a role to play in safeguarding the integrity of our sport. It's not enough to excel on the track; we must also uphold the values that make racing honorable."

Lily added, "Technology can be a powerful ally in ensuring

transparency. We should invest in systems that detect and deter unethical behavior."

The public response was overwhelmingly positive. Fans rallied behind Jake and his team, applauding their commitment to change.

One evening, as Jake was leaving the team's headquarters, he received another message from the unknown number.

Elena Martinez: Thank you for your support. Together, we can make a difference.

He smiled, replying: *Thank you for your courage. Stay safe.*

Just then, his phone rang. It was Victor Reynolds, calling from prison.

"To what do I owe this call?" Jake answered coolly.

Victor's voice was strained. "Enjoying your moment in the sun, Turner?"

"I'm surprised they allow you phone privileges," Jake retorted.

Victor sneered. "Don't get too comfortable. There are forces at play you can't begin to comprehend."

"Your threats are empty, Victor," Jake replied. "The truth is out, and justice is coming."

Victor chuckled darkly. "We'll see about that."

The line went dead.

Jake took a deep breath, contemplating the conversation. He decided to inform Detective Mitchell about the call.

She was concerned. "I'll ensure that his communications are restricted. But be vigilant. There may be others who share his agenda."

"Understood," Jake said. "We'll keep our guard up."

Despite the lingering threats, progress was evident. New leadership within the racing commission implemented stricter regulations, increased oversight, and established an independent ethics committee.

The next race was approaching—a symbolic fresh start for the sport. Jake and his team prepared diligently, hopeful that this marked the beginning of a new era.

On race day, the atmosphere was different. There was a renewed sense of optimism among drivers, teams, and fans alike.

As Jake settled into *The Phoenix*, Emma's voice came through his earpiece. "Ready to make history?"

He grinned. "Let's show them what honest racing looks like."

The race unfolded without incident. The competition was fierce but fair, and the crowd's enthusiasm was electric.

Crossing the finish line in second place, Jake felt a sense of fulfillment that went beyond podium standings. This was about more than a single race—it was about reclaiming the soul of the sport.

In the post-race interviews, he expressed his gratitude.

"Today's race was a testament to what we can achieve when we prioritize integrity and respect. I'm proud to be part of this community."

That evening, the team celebrated quietly, reflecting on the journey that had brought them here.

"Do you think we've truly turned a corner?" Sarah asked, sipping her drink.

"I believe so," Emma replied. "But we must remain committed to these values every day."

Lily nodded. "Change is a process, not a single event. But we've made significant strides."

Jake raised his glass. "To everyone who fought for what's right—known and unknown. May we continue to honor their efforts."

They toasted, the clinking of glasses a harmonious note in the backdrop of their shared resolve.

As the night wore on, Jake stepped outside, gazing up at the stars. His phone buzzed with a final message from Elena.

Elena Martinez: The phoenix rises from the ashes. Thank you for being the spark.

He smiled, typing a reply: *Thank you for giving us wings.*

Pocketing his phone, Jake felt a profound sense of peace. The challenges had been great, but so too were the victories. With steadfast allies and a collective commitment to integrity, the future of racing looked brighter than ever.

He returned inside to join his team, ready to embrace whatever came next—with open hearts, unshakable principles, and the knowledge that together, they could overcome any obstacle.

Chapter 25: The Aftermath

The sun cast a subdued glow over the paddock at the Silverstone Circuit, its usual buzz dampened by an air of uncertainty. News of the widespread arrests had spread like wildfire, leaving the racing community reeling. Teams huddled together, whispers of disbelief and betrayal filling the spaces where laughter and friendly rivalry once prevailed.

Jake Turner stood outside his team's garage, gazing at the flurry of activity as law enforcement officials moved in and out of various team headquarters. The gravity of the situation weighed heavily on him. He had fought tirelessly to expose the corruption, but seeing the reality unfold was both satisfying and heartbreaking.

Emma approached, her expression mirroring his somber mood. "They've just taken Marco Silva into custody," she informed him quietly.

Jake sighed. "I can't believe how deep this runs. Drivers, team managers, officials... it's like a bad dream."

Lily joined them, her tablet in hand. "The media is in a frenzy. Every outlet is covering the story nonstop. Fans are demanding answers."

"Good," Jake said firmly. "They deserve the truth."

Sarah and Luis emerged from the garage, their faces etched with concern. "Our sponsors are pulling out," Sarah reported. "They're distancing themselves from the sport until things settle."

Emma crossed her arms. "Can't say I blame them. This scandal has tainted everything."

Jake nodded thoughtfully. "Maybe this is the wake-up call we all needed. It's painful, but necessary."

As they stood together, a group of reporters approached cautiously. "Mr. Turner, can we get a comment?" one of them asked.

Jake exchanged a glance with Emma and Lily before stepping forward. "I'll make a brief statement," he agreed.

Microphones and cameras were hastily set up as more journalists gathered.

"Thank you all for being here," Jake began, his voice steady but somber. "The events of the past few days have shaken the very foundation of our sport. Like many of you, I am deeply saddened and angered by the revelations of corruption that have come to light.

"But I believe in the resilience of our community. This is an opportunity to rebuild, to ensure that racing embodies the principles of fairness, integrity, and passion that drew us all here in the first place.

"I urge everyone—fans, teams, officials—to come together and support the efforts to cleanse our sport of these injustices. Only then can we move forward and restore the trust that has been broken."

A reporter called out, "Do you think racing will ever recover from this?"

Jake considered the question. "Yes, I do. But it will take time, transparency, and a collective commitment to change."

Another asked, "What are your plans moving forward?"

"I intend to continue racing," Jake affirmed. "But more

importantly, I will advocate for reforms that prevent such corruption from taking root again."

As the impromptu press conference concluded, Jake retreated with his team to their motorhome.

Inside, the atmosphere was heavy. Sarah broke the silence. "I keep thinking about all the people involved. Some of them were our friends."

Luis nodded. "It's hard to accept that they were part of this."

Emma leaned against the table. "We have to remember that not everyone knew the full extent of what was happening. Some may have been coerced or manipulated."

Lily tapped her fingers thoughtfully. "The investigations will sort out the details. Our focus should be on how we can contribute to rebuilding."

Jake looked around at his team—his friends, his family. "We can set an example," he said. "By upholding the highest standards in everything we do."

They agreed, a silent pact forming among them.

Over the next few days, the racing world grappled with the fallout. Prominent figures were arrested, including several high-ranking officials within the International Racing Federation. Charges ranged from fraud and bribery to endangerment and conspiracy.

Fans expressed a mix of outrage and sadness. Social media was flooded with messages of support for honest drivers and calls for sweeping reforms.

Jake received countless messages from supporters. One stood out—a letter from a young fan named **Emily**, who wrote:

"Dear Mr. Turner,

Thank you for standing up for what's right. You are the reason I believe in racing. Please don't give up.

Sincerely,

Emily"

He shared the letter with his team. "This is why we can't lose hope," he said softly.

Emma smiled. "She's right. We have a responsibility to the next generation."

A week later, a summit was organized, bringing together drivers, team principals, sponsors, and governing bodies. The goal was to address the crisis and develop a plan for the future.

Jake was invited to speak on behalf of the drivers who advocated for change.

Standing before the assembled group, he felt the weight of the moment. "We are at a crossroads," he began. "We can either allow this corruption to define us, or we can take decisive action to redefine our sport.

"I propose the formation of an independent ethics committee, regular audits of teams and officials, and mandatory ethics training for all participants.

"Moreover, we must foster a culture where integrity is valued above winning at any cost. It's not enough to punish wrongdoing; we must prevent it by promoting transparency and accountability."

His speech was met with a standing ovation.

The summit concluded with a unanimous agreement to implement Jake's proposals, marking a significant step toward healing and renewal.

Chapter 26: Healing Wounds

The rolling hills of the English countryside stretched out before Jake as he drove along the narrow lanes toward a quaint village nestled among the greenery. The purpose of his journey weighed heavily on his heart. He was on his way to visit the family of **Michael Grant**, a fellow driver who had tragically died in a suspicious crash earlier in the season.

Michael's death had been a catalyst for Jake's determination to expose the corruption in racing. Now, with the conspiracy unraveled, Jake sought closure—for himself and for Michael's family.

He pulled up to a modest cottage, the garden blooming with late-summer flowers. Taking a deep breath, he approached the front door and knocked gently.

A woman opened the door, her eyes reflecting a mixture of curiosity and sorrow. "Mr. Turner?" she asked softly.

"Yes," Jake replied. "Mrs. Grant, thank you for seeing me."

She offered a faint smile. "Please, call me Anne. Come in."

He entered the cozy home, the scent of freshly brewed tea welcoming him. "I appreciate you taking the time to meet with me," he said.

Anne gestured toward the sitting room. "Michael spoke highly of you. He admired your integrity."

Jake felt a lump in his throat. "He was a great driver and an even better person. His loss is deeply felt."

They sat down, and Anne poured tea into delicate china cups. "I heard about everything you've done—the corruption you helped expose."

Jake nodded. "I wanted to tell you in person that Michael's death was not in vain. We discovered that his accident was a result of sabotage orchestrated by the very people we've brought to justice."

Anne's eyes glistened with tears. "I suspected as much, but no one would listen."

"I'm so sorry," Jake said earnestly. "If I had acted sooner—"

She held up a hand. "You did what you could. Michael wouldn't want you to carry that burden."

They sat in silence for a moment, the weight of shared grief hanging between them.

"Michael loved racing," Anne said finally. "But he loved the purity of it—the challenge, the camaraderie. It's comforting to know that you're fighting to preserve that."

Jake offered a small smile. "That's the goal. To honor his memory by ensuring that others don't suffer the same fate."

She reached out and placed her hand over his. "Thank you, Jake. For your courage and for coming here today."

He met her gaze. "If there's ever anything I can do for you or your family, please don't hesitate to ask."

Anne nodded appreciatively. "Actually, there is something. Michael's younger brother, **Thomas**, dreams of becoming a driver. But after everything that's happened, he's uncertain."

"Maybe I could talk to him," Jake suggested. "Offer guidance or mentorship."

"That would mean the world to him," she said, a glimmer of hope in her eyes.

Later that afternoon, Jake met with Thomas in the family's garage, where an old go-kart sat covered in a tarp.

"Mind if I take a look?" Jake asked.

Thomas shrugged, his teenage demeanor guarded. "Sure."

Jake pulled back the tarp, revealing the well-worn vehicle. "Did you and Michael work on this together?"

"Yeah," Thomas admitted. "He taught me everything."

"He must have been a great teacher," Jake said. "Would you like to take it for a spin?"

Thomas glanced at him skeptically. "It's probably rusted solid."

"Nothing a little elbow grease can't fix," Jake replied with a grin.

They spent the next few hours tuning up the go-kart, the tension gradually easing as Thomas opened up about his brother.

"Michael always said racing was about more than speed," Thomas shared. "He said it was about heart."

Jake nodded. "He was right. And with people like you carrying on that spirit, the sport has a bright future."

Thomas looked thoughtful. "Do you really think so?"

"I do," Jake affirmed. "And if you're willing, I'd be happy to help you on that journey."

A small smile crept onto Thomas's face. "I'd like that."

As evening approached, Jake prepared to depart. Anne walked him to his car. "You have a gift, you know," she said.

"What's that?" he asked.

"Inspiring others," she replied. "Giving them hope."

He shrugged modestly. "I'm just trying to do what's right."

She placed a hand on his arm. "Sometimes, that's the hardest thing of all."

He smiled gently. "Thank you, Anne. Today has meant a lot to me."

"To us as well," she said. "Safe travels, Jake."

Driving away, Jake felt a sense of peace. The visit had been healing, a chance to pay his respects and forge a new connection.

Returning to his own family home, Jake found his parents and sister waiting for him.

"How did it go?" Margaret asked, concern evident.

"It was good," Jake replied. "Emotional, but necessary."

Robert nodded approvingly. "Proud of you, son."

Jenna hugged him. "You look happier."

He smiled. "I feel like a weight has been lifted."

They settled into the living room, the warmth of family enveloping him.

Margaret spoke softly. "You know, Jake, you've grown so much through all of this."

He looked at her inquisitively. "How do you mean?"

"You've faced incredible challenges, but you've remained true to yourself," she explained. "That's something rare and precious."

He considered her words. "I couldn't have done it without the support of all of you."

Jenna grinned. "So what's next for the great Jake Turner?"

He chuckled. "Well, there's a new season ahead, with a lot of changes. But I'm excited about the possibilities."

Robert raised an eyebrow. "Thinking about mentoring any promising young drivers?"

Jake smiled knowingly. "As a matter of fact, yes."

Over the following weeks, Jake balanced his preparations for the upcoming season with his commitment to fostering new talent. He began working with Thomas Grant, introducing him to the world of professional racing in a responsible and nurturing way.

Emma and the team embraced the mentorship program, seeing it as an extension of their mission to promote integrity in the sport.

One afternoon, as they watched Thomas complete a successful test run, Lily remarked, "You're building quite a legacy, Jake."

He shrugged lightly. "Just trying to make a difference where I can."

She smiled. "Isn't that what legacies are made of?"

He pondered her words, a sense of contentment settling in. "I suppose you're right."

As the new season kicked off, there was a palpable shift in the racing community. The shadows of corruption had given way to a renewed focus on fairness and camaraderie. Drivers greeted each other with genuine respect, teams collaborated on safety initiatives, and fans returned with enthusiasm, hopeful for what lay ahead.

In the first race of the season, Jake took to the track with a clear mind and a full heart. The roar of the engine, the thrill of the chase—it all felt new again, untainted by the darkness of the past.

Crossing the finish line in a respectable position, he felt a surge of joy not just for himself but for the collective victory of everyone who had fought for this moment.

Back in the paddock, he was greeted by Thomas, beaming with excitement. "You were amazing out there!"

"Thanks, Thomas," Jake replied. "Your turn will come soon

enough."

As the sun set on the horizon, painting the sky with hues of orange and pink, Jake stood among his friends and family, a sense of fulfillment washing over him.

Healing wounds was not a quick or easy process, but step by step, they were moving forward—together.

He raised a bottle of water in a toast. "To new beginnings, and to honoring those who brought us here."

They joined in, voices united.

The journey had been arduous, but the destination was worth it. With the past acknowledged and the future embraced, Jake Turner looked ahead with hope, ready to write the next chapter of his life—on and off the track.

Chapter 27: New Horizons

The morning sun streamed through the windows of Jake Turner's apartment, casting a warm glow on the collection of racing memorabilia adorning the shelves. Trophies, photographs, and helmets—all reminders of his journey—gleamed softly. Yet, despite the symbols of success surrounding him, Jake felt a restlessness he couldn't quite name.

Since the exposure of the corruption scandal and his championship victory, Jake had become a household name. Offers from top racing teams around the world flooded in, each more enticing than the last.

Emma sat across from him at the kitchen table, a stack of proposals between them. "This one is from **Titan Racing**," she said, sliding the glossy folder toward him. "They're offering a leading position with complete creative control over the car's development."

Jake glanced at the offer without much enthusiasm. "That's generous," he acknowledged.

"Generous?" Emma echoed, raising an eyebrow. "Jake, this is what we've been working toward for years. These are the kinds of opportunities that come once in a lifetime."

He leaned back in his chair, rubbing his temples. "I know, but... I don't know if it's what I want anymore."

She studied him thoughtfully. "What's going on? Ever since the final race, you've been distant."

He sighed, gazing out the window at the city skyline. "When I started racing, it was all about the thrill, the competition, the love of the sport. But after everything that's happened—the corruption, the losses, the danger—I'm starting to wonder if this is still my dream."

Emma reached across the table, her hand resting on his. "Dreams can change, Jake. There's no shame in that."

Just then, his phone buzzed with a message from Lily. *"Meet me at our usual spot when you have time. Need to talk."*

"Is that Lily?" Emma asked.

"Yeah," he replied, standing up. "Maybe she can help me sort this out."

At a quiet café tucked away from the bustling streets, Jake found Lily waiting at an outdoor table. She looked up as he approached, a warm smile lighting up her face.

"Hey," she greeted.

"Hey," he replied, taking a seat. "You wanted to talk?"

She nodded, stirring her coffee absently. "I've been offered a new position—leading a global initiative on cybersecurity and ethics. It involves a lot of travel and working with international organizations."

"That's amazing," Jake said genuinely. "You deserve it."

"Thanks," she replied softly. "But it means I'd have to leave soon and be away for quite a while."

He felt a pang of something he couldn't quite identify. "Have you made a decision?"

"Not yet," she admitted. "I wanted to talk to you first."

"Me? Why?"

She took a deep breath. "Because you're a part of the reason I'm considering it. We've been through so much together, and I value our partnership—both professionally and personally."

He met her gaze, realizing the depth of what she was saying. "Lily, I..."

Before he could continue, she added, "I know you've been receiving offers too. Top teams, big contracts. It's a lot to think about."

He nodded. "It is. But honestly, I'm not sure if returning to the racing circuit is what I want anymore."

Her eyes searched his. "What do you want?"

"I'm still figuring that out," he confessed. "But I know that whatever I do next, I want it to be meaningful. To make a real difference."

She smiled gently. "Maybe we can find that meaning together."

He considered her words, a sense of clarity beginning to form. "Are you suggesting we embark on a new journey?"

"Why not?" she said, a hint of excitement in her voice. "We make a good team. Think about what we could accomplish beyond the track."

He felt a weight lift off his shoulders. "You know, that sounds like exactly what I need."

"Really?" she asked, her eyes brightening.

"Really," he affirmed. "Let's explore these new horizons together."

Over the next few days, Jake met with Emma and the rest of the team to discuss his decision.

"I've decided not to accept any of the offers," he announced during a team meeting.

Emma looked at him thoughtfully. "You're sure about this?"

He nodded. "I am. Racing has been an incredible part of my life, but it's time for me to move on."

Sarah leaned forward. "What will you do instead?"

"I'm going to work with Lily on global initiatives—using our experiences to promote ethics, integrity, and positive change."

Luis grinned. "That sounds like a worthy adventure."

Emma smiled softly. "We'll miss you on the track, but I understand."

"Thank you," Jake said sincerely. "Your support means a lot."

As word of his decision spread, media outlets buzzed with speculation. Headlines ranged from *"Champion Jake Turner Retires from Racing"* to *"Turner Pursues New Challenges Off the Track."*

Fans expressed mixed emotions—sadness at his departure but admiration for his commitment to making a difference.

One evening, Jake sat with his family, sharing his plans.

Margaret Turner listened intently. "You've always followed your heart," she said proudly. "I have no doubt you'll succeed in whatever you choose to do."

Robert Turner nodded in agreement. "We're behind you all the way."

Jenna smirked playfully. "Just don't forget to visit your little sister once you become a big-time world changer."

He laughed. "Never."

As preparations for their new venture progressed, Jake and Lily spent more time together, their connection deepening.

One night, after a long day of planning, they walked along the riverbank, the city lights reflecting on the water.

"Feels like everything is falling into place," Lily mused.

"Yeah," Jake agreed. "It's exciting—and a little scary."

She glanced at him. "Scary how?"

"Stepping into the unknown," he explained. "But it's easier knowing I'm not doing it alone."

She smiled. "I'm glad you feel that way."

They stopped walking, turning to face each other.

"Lily," he began, his voice sincere, "I couldn't imagine doing this with anyone else."

Her eyes softened. "Neither could I."

A moment of understanding passed between them, the unspoken feelings finally finding space to surface.

"Here's to new horizons," she said, extending her hand.

He took it, his grip warm and reassuring. "To new horizons."

Chapter 28: The Open Road

The early morning sun painted the sky with hues of pink and gold as Jake and Lily loaded the last of their bags into the RV. The vehicle was a symbol of their new journey—practical yet full of potential for adventure.

"Ready to hit the road?" Jake asked, turning to Lily with a grin.

She adjusted her sunglasses, a spark of excitement in her eyes. "Absolutely."

They climbed into the RV, Jake taking the wheel. As they pulled away, the familiar cityscape gave way to open highways and the promise of new experiences.

Their first destination was a small town renowned for its community outreach programs. They planned to volunteer and learn from local leaders, gathering insights to apply to their own initiatives.

As miles of open road stretched before them, they settled into a comfortable rhythm.

"Remember when we first met?" Lily reminisced.

Jake chuckled. "How could I forget? You hacked into my car's telemetry to warn me about sabotage."

She laughed. "Well, I had to get your attention somehow."

"You certainly did," he agreed. "Who would have thought we'd end up here?"

"Life is full of surprises," she said thoughtfully.

They arrived in the quaint town by late afternoon, greeted by

Mr. Alvarez, the coordinator of the local youth center.

"Welcome! We're thrilled to have you here," he said warmly.

"Thank you for having us," Jake replied. "We're eager to contribute however we can."

Over the next few days, they immersed themselves in the community. Jake shared his experiences with young athletes, emphasizing the importance of integrity and perseverance.

Lily conducted workshops on technology and its potential for positive impact, captivating the students with her passion.

One evening, after a successful event, they sat under a starlit sky, the sounds of laughter and music drifting from a nearby festival.

"This feels right," Lily said softly. "Being here, making a difference."

Jake looked at her, admiration evident in his gaze. "I couldn't agree more."

She met his eyes. "Jake, there's something I've been meaning to tell you."

He felt his heartbeat quicken. "What is it?"

She hesitated for a moment before taking a deep breath. "These past weeks have been incredible, and it's made me realize how much you mean to me."

He smiled gently. "You've become an important part of my life too."

She reached out, her hand finding his. "I want us to be more than partners in this journey."

He squeezed her hand, warmth spreading through him. "So do I."

They shared a tender kiss, the world around them fading away.

When they parted, she whispered, "Here's to the open road and the adventures ahead."

"To us," he added, contentment settling over them.

Their travels continued, each stop bringing new connections and opportunities. They visited schools, community centers, and organizations, spreading messages of hope and empowerment.

In a coastal village, they helped establish a program for sustainable fishing practices. In a bustling city, they collaborated on a tech initiative to bridge the digital divide.

Their relationship blossomed, the challenges and triumphs of their work strengthening their bond.

One afternoon, while driving through a picturesque landscape of rolling hills and vineyards, Lily turned to Jake.

"I've been thinking," she began.

"About what?" he asked, glancing at her with curiosity.

"About finding a place to call home base," she said. "Somewhere we can return to between projects."

He considered this. "Any ideas?"

"Actually, yes," she replied. "Remember that town where we

helped set up the youth center? They offered us a place to stay if we ever wanted to settle for a bit."

A smile spread across his face. "I like that idea. It felt like home there."

"Then let's do it," she said decisively.

Months later, they found themselves settling into a charming cottage overlooking the town. The community welcomed them with open arms, grateful for their ongoing involvement.

Jake continued mentoring young athletes, while Lily expanded her tech programs.

Their friends visited often. Emma arrived one weekend, delighted to see them thriving.

"You two have created something really special here," she remarked over dinner.

"It's been a joint effort," Jake said. "We couldn't have done it without the support of everyone."

Lily raised her glass. "To friendship and new beginnings."

They toasted, the clinking of glasses a harmonious note in their shared journey.

One evening, as they watched the sunset from their porch, Jake turned to Lily.

"Do you ever miss the rush of racing?" he asked.

She thought for a moment. "Sometimes. But then I think about all we've accomplished, and I wouldn't trade it for anything."

He nodded. "Me neither."

She leaned her head on his shoulder. "What's next for us?"

He wrapped his arm around her. "Whatever we want it to be. The open road is still out there, and there are plenty of adventures waiting."

She smiled contentedly. "As long as we're together."

"Always," he promised.

They sat in comfortable silence, the stars emerging one by one.

The journey that began on the track had led them to places they never imagined—both in the world and within themselves.

Embracing the future with open hearts, Jake and Lily looked forward to the unwritten chapters ahead, ready to face them side by side.

About the Author

Etienne Psaila, an accomplished author with over two decades of experience, has mastered the art of weaving words across various genres. His journey in the literary world has been marked by a diverse array of publications, demonstrating not only his versatility but also his deep understanding of different thematic landscapes. However, it's in the realm of automotive literature that Etienne truly combines his passions, seamlessly blending his enthusiasm for cars with his innate storytelling abilities.

Specializing in automotive and motorcycle books, Etienne brings to life the world of automobiles through his eloquent prose and an array of stunning, high-quality color photographs. His works are a tribute to the industry, capturing its evolution, technological advancements, and the sheer beauty of vehicles in a manner that is both informative and visually captivating.

A proud alumnus of the University of Malta, Etienne's academic background lays a solid foundation for his meticulous research and factual accuracy. His education has not only enriched his writing but has also fueled his career as a dedicated teacher. In the classroom, just as in his writing, Etienne strives to inspire, inform, and ignite a passion for learning.

As a teacher, Etienne harnesses his experience in writing to engage and educate, bringing the same level of dedication and excellence to his students as he does to his readers. His dual role as an educator and author makes him uniquely positioned to understand and convey complex concepts with clarity and ease, whether in the classroom or through the pages of his books.

Through his literary works, Etienne Psaila continues to leave an indelible mark on the world of automotive literature, captivating car enthusiasts and readers alike with his insightful perspectives and compelling narratives.

Visit www.etiennepsaila.com for more.

www.ingramcontent.com/pod-product-compliance
Ingram Content Group UK Ltd.
Pitfield, Milton Keynes, MK11 3LW, UK
UKHW041844141224
452457UK00012B/643